Abandoned Joy

Bre'Yanna Mitriece

Published by Bre'Yanna Mitriece Enterprises
© 2017, Bre'Yanna Mitriece Enterprises

ISBN-13 978-0692865699
ISBN-10 0692865691ii

First Printing, July 2017

10 9 8 7 6 5 4 3 2 1

Also by Bre'Yanna Mitriece:

Falling In Love with Yourself

www.BreYannaMitriece.com

Dedication

For

The forgotten woman
The motherless and fatherless woman
The Lost woman
The hurt woman
The bitter woman
The broken woman
The woman who wants to grow
The woman who desires to be loved
The woman who wants her Joy back.

May you find the love of God and the love of self so you can finally be set Free and walk into your Greater.

"They say weeping may endure for a night, but JOY will come in the morning"

"What, JOY?"

"The only JOY I've ever had, was my name"

Chapter 1

The Beginning

"Where are you going, now?" my mother questioned my dad.

"Sheena, don't act like you don't know, you know I got a meeting at the school.", my dad yelled back.

"Yea, but you had one last night, Tony." my mother snapped back.

"Well, we're having another one tonight, they're introducing a new curriculum."

"Oh, wow. Tony, do you think I'm stupid? Who is she?"

"Don't start with me, dang! I'll be back home tonight." My dad yelled.

"You better! Don't start this mess again. I'm tired of you cheating on me Tony."

"I told you, ain't nobody cheating on you, I got a meeting at my job tonight."

"Yeah, that's what you say and what about Joy. You haven't said two words to her this week, your child needs you. Do you have any time for her?" My mother yelled to the top of her lungs.

"Don't make this about Joy, because you already know."

"I already know, what?"

"That I'm trying to be the best father I can, but you know when you got pregnant with her, I wasn't ready and I never wanted a child that soon. Your parents pushed us to get married, and I'm still trying to figure things out."

"Oh, quit the bull Tony. It's been five freaking years; when are you going to quit with the excuses and make us a priority."

"I am done, talking about this with you. I gotta go."

I ran back in my room, as I heard my father slam the front door and all I could hear was my mother crying.

I was born on October 17, 1987 in a small town down in Georgia. I was the only child to my parents; They were college sweethearts. My mom became pregnant with me their senior year of college and they got married 3 months into my mother's pregnancy.

My mother named me Joy, and she hoped that my birth would bring some Joy into her and my dad's life.

They made a decent life together, my dad was a middle school teacher and my mother was a journalist for the local paper. I remember seeing them smile and be happy, but that memory will be erased as their constant arguments became an everyday occurrence. The more my parents argued, my dad stayed home less and less.

I longed for him and I craved his love and attention but, I never received any of that because as soon as he would come home, him and my mother would start arguing and out the door he would go. I can remember, maybe three or four times, of him sneaking into my room late at night and he would read bedtime stories to me. That was all I got from him, if my mom gave him hell; he no longer considered this his home.

We were no longer a family, and my mother was no longer happy. My mother rarely smiled, her life was completely wrapped up in my dad and whatever they had going on sucked the life right up out of her and it showed.

She went from being my best buddy, my tea party partner, my Barbie doll pal, to barely interacting with me. She went from cooking dinner every night, to us ordering out every day; I lived on pizza and Chinese takeout. She stayed shut up in her room, unless she was leaving for work.

At the age of six, I started taking care of my own basic needs. I learned how to bathe myself and how to call for pizza or make a sandwich. My mother was slipping away from me; She started drinking heavily, and popping these pills daily.

As each day passed, the less and less she got up for work, which caused her to get fired; I became a mother to my own mother. I would bathe her and made sure she ate; I wanted my mother back but there was a pain she was feeling that my smile couldn't take away. My dad would come home every couple of days, he would drop off money, ask how I was doing and he would leave without giving me a hug or a kiss. We lived like this for two years.

After my eighth birthday, my parents seemed to be getting back together. My dad was back home, him and my mother were sleeping in the same bed again. There was laughter in the house and my mother was smiling yet again. My dad gave her life and I was glad he was back home, because I missed that side of her. She slowed down her drinking and started cooking again. Things were going great for a few months until things got bad one night. I was in my room watching T.V. and I could hear my dad bust through the door screaming for my mother.

"Sheena, you so stupid! Why would you show up to the PTA night acting a fool?"

I hear my mother yell back.

"Oh, you know why I showed up? Because you're a dirty bastard, you're such a bastard."

"What, the hell are you talking about? I ain't doing nothing with nobody."

My mom laughed "Oh, really? I followed you last night to your little curriculum meeting, that was mysteriously at a hotel. Oh, and I watched you get out the car and approach a white car. A man! A freaking man got out of the car, and I saw my husband kiss another freaking man. So yes, I'm upset. Yes, I'm pissed the hell off, and I wanted to get out and beat you down right then and there. Oh, but no I needed to get even. So, showing up in front of your peers was the best way I could get even and to let them know that their beloved teacher is gay. Now I know why you weren't happy with me you love penis. You love men, you love men, my husband love men, oh and I knew it, I felt for a few months that something wasn't right, because you didn't really want to touch me, I mean I could handle another woman but you want me to compete with a man, I can't do that, I'll die before I compete with another man for your love, dang Tony you like penis, you like penis over me,

WHYYYYYYYYYYYYYY!!! Am I not good enough, tell me what I need to do to make you want me, I can do what he did, better than he did, but I can't let a man take you, I'll die, Tony before I lose to a man."

I heard my mom yell and scream and then I heard her sobbing hysterically. They begin to argue back and forth an argument that brought out the worst in both. I began to hear things being thrown around.

I turned my television up, I couldn't bear to hear anymore, it sounded so bad I began to cry, I cried until my head started hurting, I wanted it to all go away, I wanted to be happy, I wanted things to be normal. I wanted my parents to love one another, I wanted them to love me. I eventually turned the T.V. down and the sound of silence rung through the house. I crept out of my room and the house was in a disarray.

Broken glass and dishes were all over the kitchen floor, and some furniture was moved out of place and I find my mom sitting in a kitchen chair. Her face was full of despair and her lip had a little blood dripping from it. Next to her was a bottle of beer and her pills was scattered across the table. She must have saw me peeking from around the corner and she motioned for me to come to her. I tip-toed over to her making sure I walked carefully so I wouldn't get glass in my feet. She pulled me close, she squeezed me tight and kissed me on my cheek, something she hadn't done in years.

"I love you, Joy, I've always loved you."

She started crying and she held me tighter and the tears started flowing from my eyes, my mother was hurt and I wished I could make the pain go away. She pulled my face away from hers and pulled me into her lap, she kissed me on the cheek again, she kissed my forehead and then she kissed me on my other cheek and lastly, she kissed me on my lips.

"I love you, Joy, always know that I loved you. Mommy is hurting, and sad, and mommy just wants this pain to go away."

"I love you, Joy." she whispered, now go to bed Joy mommy's going to be alright, O.K.?"

I got off her lap, wiped the tears from my eyes, went into my room, laid down and went to sleep.

She said she loved me, so why would she do what she did? When I got up the next morning, to go use the bathroom, there was my mother, laying in her own blood. Inside her right hand was a butcher knife; My mother slit her own throat. I called for her, but she didn't answer; She wouldn't move. I shook her so many times, but she didn't wake up. I kissed her and kissed her, but she just laid there cold, her lips were blue. I cried until a numbness took over my body. I kept trying to figure out why. I finally got the strength to grab the phone and call the police.

"Hello, What's your emergency?"

I said sobbing into the phone "I'm eight years old, my name is Joy and my mother just killed herself."

They asked a few more questions, and then I hung up. I wrapped my arms around my mother, I kissed her again and I laid there beside her and cried until the police showed up.

Chapter 2

A Grandmother's "Love"

After my mother's suicide, the state took me into their custody. They contacted my dad and gave him a chance to come and get me, but he never showed up. The last time I saw him, was the day before my mother's suicide, he didn't even bother coming to the funeral. My dad wanted to live his own life, and I guess I wasn't a part of it. My mother's parents eventually stepped in and they gained custody of me. They moved me to their home down in Columbia, SC. Their house was beautiful, and a lot bigger than our home back in Georgia. They gave me my own room and tried to make me feel at home by decorating with my favorite Disney Character.

My grandparents were old school, my grandpa went to work and my grandmother stayed home. We didn't visit them much or maybe I just don't remember, and I don't remember them coming to see us much either. I can see why we never visited, my grandmother was a mean old woman.On the weekends, she would wake me up at the crack of dawn, to clean, do laundry and help her grocery shop for Sunday's dinner. Then on Sunday's we would be in church faithfully.

My grandmother was a different woman in church, she was as sweet as pie, a side I've never saw, until we went to church.

She knew how to turn it on and off. Something I never understood. There wasn't much time for cartoons or outside play because she believed she was training me to be a woman and she would always say women needed to know how to clean, and cook. She said that I couldn't learn how to do that by watching cartoons. She drove me crazy.

My grandmother was beautiful; She was the color of caramel or maybe a little lighter. She wore her hair in a short curly afro. She was short with wide hips and large breast. I looked nothing like her or my mother, I was my daddy's child. My skin was the color of milk chocolate and my hair was long and curly. I was a little chubby, but I was tall for an eight-year-old. I often wished I looked like her and my mother, they were both beautiful and I wished I had that look.

My grandmother did what she thought was best by me. She ruled with an iron fist and was never loving. When she taught me things about life, she made a point to bring up my skin color every chance she got. I remember a time she was teaching me how to make potato salad, and well somehow, I left out the relish. She made a big deal about it and I recall her saying:

"You can't make those kind of mistakes Joy. You already a dark skin girl and you already gotta work hard to get a man to notice you. Don't make it even harder on yourself. A man wants a woman, who looks good and one that could cook, so pay attention to what I'm teaching you, just in case you can't win him with your looks, you can win him with your cooking."

Then there was this other time, she was taking me shopping for school clothes and there was this pretty yellow top that I wanted badly and I remember her saying

"You're too dark for that shirt, and to fat it just won't look right on you, child. You don't want to look like a clown, don't make things hard on yourself child. Why don't you get this white shirt?"

She really did a job on me and my self-esteem. I was too dark and too chubby to be pretty from what I got from her. I couldn't understand why she was mean and didn't like me, but I continued to do everything she asked, I really wanted her to like me, I really wanted her to love me.

A year after I was there she had me cooking dinner for my grandpa. She taught me to be a server; whatever he needed. I was at his beck and call, no matter the request. I would help her iron his clothes and I would help with running his bath; I was severely exhausted. I think my grandma forgot that I was still a child, who wanted to have fun, to play, laugh and in her home, I couldn't do any of that.

Every night I looked forward to school, that was the only place I had to myself. I loved school and I excelled at every subject. I met Shantel in my fourth-grade class and we became friends instantly.

Shantel looked a lot like my grandmother, but her hair was short and her mother styled it in individual ponytails with berets at the ends. She had chinky eyes and looked like she was Chinese. She was beautiful and I loved her. Shantel's dad had abandoned her just like my dad , and our common pain drew us closer. I finally felt like someone loved me back.

Shantel would invite me over for sleepovers, but my grandma would never let me go. She didn't trust Shantel's mother because Shantel's mother was young and already had five children out of wedlock including Shantel. She told me Shantel's mother was loose and that's not the kind of company she wanted me to keep; but Shantel loved me and I needed her. She did her best to prevent me from going over to Shantel's house, and she even beat me for asking once, so I dared not ask again.

I remember one Sunday; my grandmother was feeling ill and didn't have the strength to make it to church. It was youth Sunday and I really wanted to go, so I got up the courage to ask if I could go with Shantel and her mom. My grandmother must have confirmed it with Shantel's mother because all I remember is my grandmother yelling for me to get dressed. I rushed and got dressed. I put on my favorite pink dress and put my hair into two French braids; I was on cloud nine. Shantel could barely ring the doorbell before I went flying out the door.

Our church was small and everybody knew everybody. I was sitting on the back pew with Shantel waiting for church to start, when I overheard two women talking about my grandfather Eugene. They both were older ladies with make-up caked on their faces and they had some of the ugliest church hats I had ever seen. I snickered a bit every time I looked at them.

"Yes, honey, I think I'm in love with that Eugene. He knows how to take care of my needs" the taller lady said.

"Well, that Eugene Baker is fine child, and a good man honey." the shorter lady said.

They high-fived one another and continued talking about my grandfather. Part of me really hoped they weren't talking about my grandfather, but I knew they were. My grandfather was a charmer, he was suave and if Denzel had a twin it would be my grandfather. Every woman wanted him, but my grandmother was the lucky one who could get him to marry her. I couldn't focus at church, I was thinking about how I would break the news to my grandmother about my grandfather and the tall lady. I later found out her name was Alma Peters. I didn't say much on the car ride home, I was just ready to get home to tell my grandmother. I thanked Shantel's mother, hugged Shantel and ran inside the house.

I could smell the sweet potato pie as I walked into the kitchen where my grandmother was preparing Sunday dinner.

"How was church, Joy?" my grandmother asked.

"Church was good. Grandma, you know that Alma Peters lady? She said that she's in love with grandpa. How is she in love with grandpa when grandpa is married to you?

She gave me a look of disgust.

"Joy, now what I tell you about meddling in grown folk's business? You keep your little tail out of grown folk's business, you here?"

"But, she said she loves him, grandpa is yours, he's not hers, so why does she love him?"

"Look, child, you mind children's business, your grandfather is a good man, you here!? He works and he makes a nice living for us. He is going to be a man, and well sometimes men have other women and that's just how it is; that's how it's always been. He makes his home here with me, so leave that alone and mind children's business."

"But grand- "

"No buts child! We're done you here?! Stay in a child's place and out of grown folk's business. Children ought to be seen and not heard, now go take those clothes off, wash your hands and come help me snap these peas."

I didn't understand why my grandmother excused my grandfather for his cheating and she didn't make a fuss and she wasn't angry with my grandfather. She continued cooking dinner as if nothing happened, but my mother wasn't like that. She was always fussing at my dad for his cheating ways, but my grandmother never said one word to my grandfather about it.

That day my grandmother taught me something about men. Maybe my daddy was just being a man, doing what men do and my mother should have let him, then maybe she would have been happy and maybe she would still be here with me.

I laid in bed that night reminiscing about my mom. I missed her so much. I just wanted to feel a touch, a kiss. I wanted to feel some love. My grandmother took me in but for what, she never showed me any affection; not one kiss, not one hug. No, I love you, nothing. I was in my grandmother's home, but I didn't feel any of my grandmother's love. I cried myself to sleep that night, and every night after that. I longed to be loved by my grandmother.

Chapter 3

A Grandfather's "Love"

School was out for the summer, and I was excited about going to the local summer camp. I was even more excited because Shantel was going to be there. I was surprised my grandmother allowed me to walk to camp every day as strict as she was. I was going to be ten years old in October, and my body was already filling out. My breast was growing and my hips were stretching out, because of my height; I looked a lot older than nine. The neighborhood boys would try to hit on me every day on my way to summer camp, but I ignored them like my grandmother taught me, I could hear her now.

"Joy, these boys don't want nothing but to stick their hands in your cookie jar and you're keeping your cookie in the jar."

So, I stayed away from boys, but those boys weren't the problem. The man I lived with, the man who said he loved me, my grandfather was putting his hands in my cookie jar every day and every night. My grandfather was molesting me.

It all started a few weeks before school let out for the summer. I was drawing my grandfather's bath like I did every night, but this night was different.

My grandmother left to go to her Tuesday night bingo game and while he was relaxing in his bath, I heard him call for me. He had never done anything like this so I was reluctant to go. I stood outside the door.

"Sir!" I called out "Did I forget something?"

"Joy, come in here, I need you."

I slowly turned the door knob, I wasn't sure what to expect; I was never allowed in the bathroom while he was bathing. I walked in and covered my eyes with my hands.

"Joy, what the hell are you doing?"

"You said you needed me." my eyes were still covered.

"Child, come over this way and come wash my back."

"But, um, um, I stuttered, the-, the-, that's what grandma does."

"Is your grandma here? Get the towel and wash my back child."

I was an obedient child, so I had to do what was asked of me, or I would get beat. I uncovered my eyes, still looking away from the tub. I grabbed the towel and he handed me the soap.

"Joy, wash your pa-pa back for him tonight."

"Yes, sir."

I lathered the towel and I began to scrub his back and he started making noises, the sounds continue as I washed his back.

"Joy, you are filling out ain't cha girl? your thighs getting thick, child."

I listened to him talk about my body, but I never replied, I continue to wash his back.

"Joy come around this way, pa-pa needs you to do something else" he commanded.

"O.K., what else?" I questioned.

He grabbed his penis.

"I want you to wash this. I want you to wash this." he rubbed his penis up and down.

I got lost in my thoughts, I was confused as to why my grandfather wanted me to touch his private part.

"Joy, Joy" he called.

I came back to and realized he was still motioning for me to come and wash his penis.

"Let's go girl, this ain't nothing to be afraid of. Put the towel down, put some soap in your hands and come wash me."

I did just what he asked of me. I lathered my hands and I washed his penis and he told me to wash by going up and down, the more I moved my hands the louder the sounds became.

"Faster, child, go faster." he said.

I did just that. I went faster and faster and then suddenly, a white liquid came from his penis and was dripping all over my hands, I jumped back.

"What's your problem child? That ain't going to hurt you, now go wash your hands."

I stood up and I went to the sink to wash my hands. This didn't feel right, but my grandfather loved me. Right? I began to have mixed feelings; my grandfather wouldn't hurt me. Right? After that, he told me not to tell anyone that it was our special thing and to keep quiet, so I did.

This went on every Tuesday night for the whole summer. I didn't tell a soul. I didn't want to disappoint my grandfather. It was just between him and I. I made him feel good and he showed me his love by buying me whatever I liked. My grandmother said he was spoiling me too much.

School was back in from summer break and I was in the fifth grade. I had grown taller and I had started growing breasts. My grandfather continued to have his way with me. It never stopped, it went from Tuesday night baths to every night he would sneak in my room, when my grandmother was asleep. He would turn me over on my back and he would kiss me and that would wake me up.

The first time he said he wanted to play a little game and he told me to open my legs and I could feel his cold fingers touching my vagina. I then felt a sensation of pain, a couple of tears rolled from my eyes. His fingers were inside my vagina and it was a pain I've never felt, but it felt good at the same time. His touches confused me because my grandmother said to never let anyone touch my cookie, so why was my grandfather doing it. Confusion set in. He started kissing me and I kissed him back and it felt good. I was no longer was confused, I felt loved.

This went on for about two more years until my grandmother caught him in my room one night, and she had the audacity to be mad at me. She went off on me and she blamed me. She said that I was fast, just like my mother and she didn't want any fast tail girls in her home. I tried to plead with her and let her know it was all my grandfather; that he told me that it was our special thing.
She just wouldn't believe me, she took his side and beat me. After that day she caught us, she made sure to never leave me alone with him, but she had no control over him.

He would still sneak in my room some nights and have his way with me. Now that I had an understanding, that what he was doing was wrong, I began to hate him and her.

I hated her for not protecting me, she saw her husband hurting me and she allowed me to suffer; she abandoned me to save her marriage. I no longer cared about pleasing them.

I started to rebell against my grandparents. I became disrespectful and I stopped helping around the house. She tried to beat me, but I was too quick for her and I began to fight back. I started skipping school with Shantel and we started hanging out with the neighborhood boys. Shantel and I would perform oral sex on anybody who would ask for it; we got wild and oral sex became our thing. We got a reputation at our middle school for it, but we didn't care. In between skipping school, I started coming home late, I was planning my escape, I rather be anywhere in the world than to live another day with my grandfather.

I finally confessed everything to Shantel and we came up with a plan that I would just move in with her and her mother. We didn't tell her mother about the molestation, but instead we convinced her mom that I got into a huge fight with my grandparents and I just couldn't go back and that I didn't feel safe there. Surprisingly she believed us. I knew all my info, so she didn't need to contact them for anything. I was twelve now and I knew how to take care of myself. One day I left for school and I never looked back.

Chapter 4

"My First"

It has been about two years since I left my grandparents' home and I have seen them around at church and they would speak but I knew it was all for show. My grandmother really hated me. She always has and knowing that her husband wanted me, angered her even more. I couldn't stand to look at them, so I stopped going to church.

Ms. Ann, Shantel's mother told me that she heard from a few church members that my grandfather was extremely sick and he had a stroke. She said I should reach out to them; I told her I was but I lied. I wasn't going to reach out to people who never reached out to me and after all he's done to me he could die for all I care, both. I tried to block them out of my mind, I didn't want to give them any more energy, I wanted to move on with my life.

Shantel and I decided to get jobs at a local Taco Bell. I wanted a job so I could help Ms. Ann out; she was already providing a roof over my head, the least I could do was take care of my other needs. There was just a few weeks left in the school year and summer break was upon us. Shantel and I couldn't wait to have some fun with money in our pockets; we were up to no good.

I watched the clock move slowly; It was ten minutes left in my shift and I was ready to go. I worked from three to nine about four days out of the week and I was extremely tired. Shantel and I worked the same hours and days, that made it easy on Ms. Ann because she had to pick us up from work. I had a blast working with Shantel; we were two peas in the pod. I considered her my sister and I don't know where my life would be if I hadn't met her.

"Joy." a familiar voice called my name.

"You can clock out." my manager said.

"Thank you, Ms. Mary, see you tomorrow."

I clocked out and walked outside looking for Shantel, she was already getting into her mother's car but her mother wasn't driving, a young boy was. I was curious to know who this boy was because Ms. Ann didn't play about her BMW, she worked too hard for it so, I was shocked to see him driving it. I walked over to the car and opened the door and slid in.

"Joy, this is my cousin Michael, my mother sent him to pick us up because Maliah is sick."

"Hey, Michael, nice to meet you." I said tiredly.

"What's up Ma" he replied. He put the car in reverse turned the radio up and my song *"Down for you" by Ja Rule and Ashanti* came blasting through the speakers as we made our way to the house.

Ms. Ann had a house full of people. I shared a room with Shantel and her sister Shyanne, her other siblings had their own room. I just found out Michael was going to be staying with Ms. Ann as well. Michael was from New York and he was getting into a ton of trouble back home, so his mother felt like being out in the country would slow him down. Michael was seventeen and he wasn't that attractive, he was about 5'10 and he had a medium build. He was light skinned like Shantel and he put you in the mind of Terrance Howard but the broke version. It wasn't his looks that drew you in, he had a down to earth personality that just pulled you in closer.

I was crushing on Michael and I wanted him so bad. I would do little things like cook for him and help him with his laundry, hoping he would get the hint and make me his girlfriend. The first time I realized Michael wanted me as more than a friend, it happened when we were all sitting outside smoking weed. It was me, Shantel, Michael and Michael's homeboy Chris.

"Ya'll don't know nothing about smoking weed." Chris said.

"Whatever, you don't know nothing about smoking weed." Shantel shot back.

"This is what we do." I replied.

"Oh really, what else do you do?" Michael asked as he winked his eye at me.

I almost peed on myself. I wanted him bad, and when he winked at me I could have fainted.

"Maybe you could find out sometime." I said to Michael smirking.

"I mean what you during later, I'm tryna find out today." He laughed.

Shantel cut her eyes at Michael and then she looked at me and smiled. She knew just how much I wanted Michael.

We passed the blunt around until the blunt got short. Once we were done, Michael asked me to go for a walk with him around the neighborhood, and I happily obliged him; I was so excited. We left Shantel and Chris alone and proceeded to walk around the neighborhood.

He kept talking about how thick I was and how nice my lips were, it felt good to hear someone compliment me in a good way. As I grew, I slimmed down a bit and all the fat I carried as a child, filled into the right places.

My thighs were thick and my hips were wide, I didn't have much of a butt, it was my thighs and hips that got me attention from the boys. We ended up on a walking trail about a mile away from Shantel's house. The walking trail ran through the woods and after a while the houses were no longer in sight and we were surrounded by trees.

Once we were deep in the woods, Michael started kissing me. His kisses sent tingles down my spine and then he started feeling on my booty. I was on cloud nine, this was what I always wanted; I always wanted to get this close to him. He pulled his penis out and asked me to touch it and I did; the way I felt about him, I would do anything he asked of me. He brought up the conversation we had over weed and ask me to show him what I could do.

I pushed him up against a tree, I got on my knees and I performed oral sex on Michael in the middle of the woods, and I wouldn't have had it any other way. I wanted Michael in more ways than I thought and I just wanted to please him.

All summer long Michael and I was kicking it. We smoked weed together and I performed oral sex on him whenever he liked it. Michael did ask me for sex, but I wasn't sure I was ready for that. Michael and his boy Chris started selling weed; Shantel and I would sell weed for them.

I wanted Michael to know that I was down for him and although we never made what we were doing official, in my mind I was his and he was mine.

My emotions for him grew deeper and I would ask him a couple times why we couldn't be together. He would respond saying that I was too young, and that we should just keep things like they were. Even though I wanted more with Michael, I was willing to except whatever he gave me just to have that time with him.

Michael started doing his own thing outside of the house, he would have girls picking him up and dropping him off. That bothered me, but I didn't say anything to him about it. I continued giving him oral sex whenever he wanted, hoping he would eventually leave those girls alone. Unfortunately, it continued; he kept dealing with me and those other girls. I wanted Michael all to myself and I decided I would let him be my first. I figured that was the missing piece and if I had sex with him, he wouldn't need those other girls; I could have him all to myself. I wasn't ready for sex before, but I was more than ready to give it to him now.

I had the perfect plan put into place. Ms. Ann was at work and Shantel took the other kids to the park. Michael had no idea what was about to happen and I didn't want to give it away, so I convinced Michael that I wanted to smoke a blunt. We smoked the blunt in Shantel's room, and then I started performing oral sex. Once he started playing around with me, I let him know that we could go further. Michael laid me down and we made love; I couldn't have been any happier. He was my first and I want what we had to last forever.

∎∎∎

"There she goes right there." I yell at Shantel after seeing Michael's girlfriend at the mall.

"Ugh, I can't stand that whore, I don't even know what Michael see in her" I said to Shantel.

Her name was Ariya. She was a light skin girl, shorter than I was and she had what some would consider the perfect shape. A flat tummy, thick thighs and big butt. She had micro braids in her hair that she pulled up into a bun and she had on a red and white stripped maxi dress. Truthfully, she was a pretty girl; she was light skinned and that's probably why I couldn't stand her. I envied her and wanted to be her and I wanted Michael to want me, just like he wanted her.

After I lost my virginity to Michael, I didn't become his girlfriend like I expected. Things between him and I continued the same as they were before, sex was just added to the equation. I took pride in my vagina and knowing just how good my sex was, I just knew my sex would win him over, but it didn't. That hurt me, but not as much as his confession of him having a girlfriend and that he wanted to be faithful to her. I was so crushed and hurt. I tried to do any and everything in my power to try to get him to recognize how good of a girl I would be to him, but none of that mattered, she had something I just didn't.

"Shantel, I should go punch her in her face with those ugly braids in her hair." I said angrily.

"Joy, don't even sweat her. Let her have Michael he's probably going to cheat on her anyway." Shantel replied.

"Ugh!!!! I just can't stand her, just let me walk pass and bump into her, I promise I won't say nothing."

"Joy, just don't start no mess!"

We walked over to the kiosk where she was trying on sunglasses. I bumped into her causing her to drop a pair of sunglasses onto the floor.

I laughed, "That's what that whore gets. Now she has to pay for those sunglasses she broke."

I was hurt to the core. Michael just threw me away when little Ms. Ariya came into his life. It broke me down and tore away at my self-esteem because, I felt like I gave him all that he needed, and there was still something about me that wasn't good enough.

Michael eventually moved in with his girlfriend and after all my attempts at trying to break them up, it seemed to only keep them together and it made Michael dislike me even more.

I finally realized that I wasn't who he wanted; maybe I just wasn't pretty enough, maybe I wasn't light enough or maybe her sex was better than mine. I realized that she did something for Michael that I couldn't do and I had to realize that I wasn't Ariya. Michael was my first love, my first heartbreak and knowing he would never see me as his girlfriend was one of the toughest pill I ever had to swallow.

Chapter 5

"Basketball and Boys"

After everything that happened with Michael, Shantel offered to cheer me up by asking me to go with her to a basketball game at the school. Our school's basketball games were like concerts; loud music, the crowd was hyped, it was the place to be on a Friday Night. I decided to take her up on her offer because she wasn't going to take no for an answer. It was the middle of November and I wanted to dress cute, something I hadn't done in a while. I put on a navy-blue sweater and a pair of dark blue jeans and some white air forces. My clothes hugged my body just the way I liked and I pulled my hair back into a low bun. I accented my outfit with two of my silver necklaces that stopped right above my cleavage and a pair of medium sized silver hoop earrings.

I had a blast at the game, after all the crying I've been doing behind Michael, this game was just what I needed. After the game Shantel talked about going to a house party. I really didn't feel up to it, but I knew Shantel wouldn't let me go back home, so I guess I was going. As we were walking out of the gym a cutie pie yelled Shantel's name.

"Shantel, yo what's up." cutie pie asked.

I looked at her with a smirk on my face.

"Who is that?" I whispered.

"Just come on girl, I'll introduce you." she said pulling me over to the cutie pie.

Cutie pie was tall. He had to be at least 6 feet something and he was the color of butterscotch candy. He had almond shaped eyes and the perfect white teeth, he reminded me of Ginuwine. I noticed he had on one of our school's basketball jersey's, he was a player on the team. I looked him over a couple of times and he was fine.

"Is this you?" I whispered to Shantel.

"Something like that, you know how I do." she chuckled.

"Oh, Ima get you, keeping secrets and all." I replied to her.

"Desmond, this is my sister Joy, Joy this is Des."

"Nice to meet you Des."

"Nice to meet you too, Joy."

"Dang, Shantel you didn't tell me you had a sister that looked like her." Des said looking in my direction.

"I told you she was cute and that's all you needed to know."

"So, yall going to the after party at Mark's crib?" Des asked.

"Yea we're going." Shantel said.

"Bet, I want to do some things to you." Desmond said to Shantel.

"Oh, you will." she said laughing.

They joked and talked a little bit more and then another cutie walked up and dapped up Desmond.

"Yo, bro you ready to go." he asked Des.

"Yea, aye Shantel you got a ride to Mark's crib?" Des inquired.

"We were gonn- "

"Naw ya'll can ride with us." Des said, interrupting Shantel.

Shantel face lit up.

"Oh, my bad, Jamier, you know Shantel and this is her sister Joy." Des said.

   He reached out to shake my hand and oh my goodness he was handsome. He looked a little bit like Omarion from that group B2K; He had cornrows braided straight back.

32

He was just as tall as Desmond, but he was a little slimmer. I could stare at him all day, I regained my focus and shook his hand back.

"Nice to meet you." I said nervously.

We all hopped into Desmond's black *Nissan* Maxima and we spun over to Mark's crib. I didn't say much during the car ride over. The boys were getting crunk and drinking a little bit of liquor before we pulled up to the party. Mark didn't stay on the best part of town so the boys reassured us if anything popped off that they had our back, which made Shantel and I feel safe.
    We walked inside the party and it was jumping. You could smell the scent of marijuana in the air and everybody had red cups in their hands, all the girls were grinding on boys to *Lil Jon's "Get Low"*.
 A couple of the girls were very excited to see Desmond and Jamier, but because we walked in with them, the girls turned their noses up at us; I paid it no mind. Shantel and Desmond got lost in the party and I found my way to an empty seat in the corner in Mark's living room. I noticed Jamier over in a corner talking to some brown skin girl. Even though the music was flowing, I was ready to go. Shantel finally found her way back to me and she handed me a drink.

"Here take this and loosen up girl." Shantel said.

She handed me the cup.

"This party is off the hook! It's some cuties up in here and you over here sitting in the corner. Go have you some fun."

"Naw. I'm good girl, I'm just chilling." I responded.

"You tripping, about Michael again?"

"Naw, Shantel, I'm good. I just feel like chilling, I'll dance in a few."

"Yea, ok. Well Des told me that Jamier wants to get with you."

"If he was feeling me, then why he all up in her face?" I pointed to the brown skin girl and Jamier.

"Girl, don't sweat that. That's his ex, she always in his face, she's definitely not important."

"Yea, ok."

"Give him a chance, he a real cool dude and why not talk to him so you could get over Michael."

Nelly's "Hot in Here" came on and before I could respond to Shantel, she pulled me by the arm and dragged me to the dance floor. As reluctant as I was, I decided to let down my hair after all this was my jam. Everybody was dancing, it literally got hot up in Mark's Living Room.

I was grinding my body and a few dudes tried to come behind me and dance, but I pushed them off. Then I felt the warmth of another body behind me and I was getting ready to push him off, I noticed it was Jamier. My stomach dropped. He started moving with me, which I liked. I guess he wanted it, so I made sure to give him what he came for. I could see little Miss Brown Skin giving us the look but I didn't care, I pretended he was my man and I enjoyed every moment of our dance. Jamier and I danced to a couple more songs until I worked up a sweat and needed a break. I walked outside to cool down and to my surprise Jamier followed behind.

"After all that dancing, I could see why you need a break." he said joking.

"I see you liked it." I shot back.

"And what if I did." he said smirking flashing those pretty white teeth.

"I mean, you have the right to." I said confidently.

We stood outside talking for a good twenty minutes or so. He was a senior at our school and an All- American Athlete. He was a star on the team and he was recruited by USC to play for them in the fall. He lives at home with both of his parents and his two younger sisters. He asked me about my parents, I told him they died in a car crash; I left it at that and continue inquiring about him.

He talked about his dreams after high school; he wanted to play college ball and he eventually wanted to go to the NBA. He was very smart and sweet. He asked me did I hear any rumors about him and if I did don't believe them because people like to lie on him. I never heard of him and that was because I didn't get caught up in the drama at the school. I went to school did what I needed to do and I would go to work and then home, but I did want to know more about him. He was very impressive, he had real dreams, and unlike Michael who wanted to just sell weed and rap, Jamier had a real future. For a second he made me think of my future, but at this point in my life I just wanted to be in love and I wanted someone to love me back.

"What ya'll doing out here." Shantel said interrupting Jamier and I.

"Just coolin." he replied.

I flashed a smile to let her know I was good.

"Jamier, so you trying to get with Joy?" Shantel asked with no inhibitions.

"I mean, I think she cool and I would like to get to know her more." he replied.

"Sooo, are you going to give her your number?"

"Dang, Shan can I get to that?" he said.

36

"I'm just saying, she doesn't have time for no games.

"I got this. Let me handle this, where Des at anyway." Jamier replied trying to change the subject.

"Oh, yea that's why I came out here. Des ready to go, he done messed around and drunk too much, he done already threw up on Mark couch."

"Wow, yea let me go get that dude." Jamier said.

"You ready?" Jamier asked me.

"Yeah, we can go." I said.

    Jamier ended up driving Desmond's car and Shantel insisted that I sit in the passenger seat next to Jamier. The entire car ride home we talked a little bit more about some of our likes and dislikes. We decided to exchanged numbers. When we pulled up to Shantel's house. I hugged him and let him know I would call him tomorrow.
    After we got in and got ourselves situated, we stayed up a little bit longer talking about the night and the boys. She let me know that she kept Desmond a secret because of how bad I was feeling about Michael and she didn't want to seem like she was throwing him in my face.
    She said she just began talking to Desmond two months ago and that she really liked him.

I let her know how I was feeling about Jamier and how I hoped him and I could become a couple because I really liked him. We laughed about double dating and being in love.

Before falling asleep, I couldn't help but be thankful that Shantel got me out the house. I was so happy that I met Jamier. He was fine and a gentleman. Maybe he'll be the one to love me.

Chapter 6

"The Burning"

"Oh, you look so pretty, you should get that one. The turquoise looks pretty on your skin." I said to Shantel.

We were out shopping for prom dresses. We were invited to the senior prom by Desmond and Jamier. We were more than excited to go.

Jamier and I have been in an official relationship for the past six months and I was beyond happy to be his girlfriend. Although we had a few bumps in the road, I wouldn't trade it for nothing. I finally won I was finally someone's girlfriend, and I wasn't going to let anyone take that from me. He loved me and made that known to me and everyone else. Desmond and Shantel, while they had a good little friendship they had their share of drama and him cheating on her. She would always say that I needed to keep my eye on Jamier because if Desmond was doing it, Jamier was too. I insisted that I knew my man and Jamier would never do anything like that to hurt me, he was different. I could see the jealousy at times because Desmond didn't do half the things Jamier did, but she wouldn't leave him alone. He had hopes of an NBA future and she wanted to ride it out with him.

About a week into our relationship I decided to have sex with Jamier. He said he loved me and our sex just put the icing on the cake. From the very beginning we never used condoms, he said he never liked the way they felt. He insisted I get on the pill and I did; with everything he had going on, he didn't want a baby and I could understand that. I also stopped smoking weed when I got with Jamier, he wasn't into that and he didn't want me to do it either. I didn't want to do anything he didn't like. I wanted to make him happy, he considered me something special and I wanted it to stay that way forever.

"O.K girl are you going to get it or not, because I have to go to the bathroom." I said to Shantel as she twirled around in her prom dress.

"Yeah, I'ma get it. Go ahead and go to the bathroom, I'll be finished when you get back."

"Alright." I responded.

I rushed to the bathroom, I had to go bad, I could no longer hold it. I lined the toilet and positioned myself in front of the toilet and began to squat, it rushed out and it burned. It hurt so bad, the pain was horrible.

"What in the world?" I thought to myself and when I looked down at my panties, it was full of yellow-like discharge. I got myself together and prepared to wash my hands.

My mind went into overload, I didn't know what was going on. My vagina was on fire and I needed some answers.

I walked out of the bathroom and Shantel was standing outside waiting for me.

"You good?" she asked noticing my screwed-up face.

"Girl, I went to pee and the mess was burning and it hurt so bad." I replied.

"Well, maybe you got a UTI, or it could be a yeast infection. We could go get some cream when we leave from here."

"Yea, let's do that. This mess got to go today."

We left the mall and made our way to a local drug store. I bought an over the counter yeast infection cream and one for UTI.

It has been a week now and neither one of those over the counter medicines worked. Shantel insisted that it must be something more, and I was starting to feel the same way. Deep down I didn't want her to be right because I didn't want Jamier to be like Desmond, I hoped Jamier wasn't like Desmond.
I pushed my pride to the side and asked Shantel to go with me to the local health department. I was so embarrassed sitting up in the clinic. Everyone looking at me like I did something wrong. I was so grateful for Shantel coming with me, I don't know if I could of did it alone.

"B4? Follow me." an older white nurse with short hair said as I got up to follow her to the back. She did the STD test on me and told me to give them a call in a week to get my results back. She did give me a prescription for Chlamydia based upon my symptoms; I can't believe I had an STD, and that meant Jamier was cheating on me. My heart felt like it was burning. I could've cried, my good man turned out to be just like everyone said he was. Shantel noticed me coming from the back. She got up to meet me.

"So, what they say?" she said as we walked out of the clinic.

"They said to give them a call in a week, but she said it maybe Chlamydia and she gave me this prescription for it."

"Are you serious, Joy? Oh dang, girl I'm sorry. I told you that needed to keep watch over Jamier, him and Des are just the same."

Even though I didn't want her to know, I no longer cared, I had bigger fish to fry and that was confronting Jamier.

"I guess you were right, Shan. I just can't believe he would do something like this. He promised me he wasn't out here doing me like Des was doing you, but I guess he was. Can you take me by his house?"

"Sure. You going to be ok?"

"Yea after I cuss him out." I said trying not to cry.

We hopped into Shantel's 1992 Honda Civic, that she bought with her Taco Bell money and made our way over to Jamier's house.

On the car ride over I played over and over in my mind how I was going to confront him, but when we pulled up, I was numb. I couldn't even get out.

"Are you sure you're ready to do this?" Shantel asked.

"Um, yea, girl Ima do it." I replied.

I put my hand on the door handle, opened the door and slid out and walked up to Jamier's House. I had knots in my stomach and even though I was mad, I was slightly nervous.

"What if he thinks you cheated on him?" "What if the results are negative?" "What if he wants to break up?"

These questions played over and over in my head as I rang the doorbell. Just my luck, Jamier answered the door and was looking good. He had on a black wife beater, and some red and black basketball shorts. He stepped outside and closed the door.

"Hey, baby, what are you doing here?" he asked as he kissed me on my lips.

"I missed you baby." I said nervously as I gave him a hug. He smelled so good.

"Babe, you good, what's going on? You ain't never pop up like this." he asked with concern.

"Baby, I haven't been feeling well lately, I..."

He interrupted.

"You aren't pregnant, are you? I thought you were taking your pills! Man come on now, tell me you ain't pregnant."

I snapped "I am taking my pills and no I'm not pregnant."

"So, what is it then Joy." he said with a puzzled look on his face.

"I've been hurting lately, like really bad and my vagina been burning. I just left the clinic and they said I may have Chlamydia."

"Oh, word? Wow, wow. Joy, I got to tell you something, but promise you won't be mad"

"What, is it Jamier?" I asked a little irritated.

"I'm sorry, I messed up big time. A couple weeks ago, you know when me and the boys went down to Miami for spring break?

Well one night we had a hotel party and I got tore up and there was this chick there and I guess one thing led to another. We ended up having sex and she must've burnt me. I'm sorry, I didn't know how to tell you." his eyes started watering up.

Seeing him tear up let me know that he was truly remorseful for what he has done, my anger faded and somehow I felt the need to comfort him.

"It's ok, you know you have to protect yourself. You can't sleep with hoes unprotected."

"You right babe, I was drunk, I didn't remember. You forgive me boo? Please don't make me use condoms." he pulled me close to him and embraced me.

"Yea, I forgive you and no I won't make you."
I wanted to be mad, but he was honest and I respected an honest man. He made a mistake, we all make mistakes, he said he loved me so why would I leave him over his mistake?

Chapter 7

"The Main Chick"

The last bell rung to commence the end of my sophomore year, and I was ready for the Summer. This summer I planned on working and hanging with my girl and my man. After the little incident, he tried his best to show me he wasn't cheating, but I just didn't trust him and my insecurities would get the best of me. There would be times he would say he was one place and word would get back to me that he was at another place. Which caused us to have arguments daily. He claimed he loved me and wouldn't hurt me again, I just didn't believe him, but leaving him was out of the question. I rather have some of him, than none of him. He was just doing what men do anyhow.

I walk over to my locker to clean it out and I noticed a piece of paper taped to it. I got a little excited *"What is he up to now?"* I thought to myself. I pulled the note off my locker and opened it, my stomach dropped.

Joy,

Ask your man about Miami
I figured You should know
Kierra

My body tensed up and my heart rate increased. I was getting angry.

"Ask my man about Miami? What the hell is she talking about?" my mind wondered.

Kierra was Jamier's ex, the brown skin girl at the party. Kierra and I exchanged a few words on several different occasions, but Jamier reassured me that she was just jealous of him and I.

"How did they link up in Miami, is she the girl that burnt him?" My mind started wondering.

I was burning hot. There were so many thoughts dancing through my head. I just wished she would leave me and my man alone. I stuffed what I could from my locker into my bookbag and went looking for her. I went to the Senior Parking Lot and there she was leaned up against her raggedy *Toyota Corolla*, talking to a couple of girls. If she never felt my wrath before she was about to feel it.

I walked up to her and she looked at me and said "Did you ask your man about Miami?" her friends started laughing and I lost my cool; I punched her right in the face. I must have blacked out, and all I remember was Jamier holding me back and fussing at me to get in his car.

"Yo, chill out Joy! Why you out here acting like this? Out here fighting acting like a ghetto girl."

I paid little attention to what he said. I was looking for a way to get back over to Kierra. I scanned the parking lot but I didn't see her.

"Yo, get in the car." he pulled the car door opened and tried to make me get in. "Get in!!" he yelled.

I got into the car, but I was still pissed and I wanted to punch Jamier in the face. I can't believe he did me that way.

"Yo, you can't be acting like that."

"How am I supposed to act? You got this chick acting like I'm the side chick! So, what went down in Miami?" I snapped.

"Man, ain't nothing go down in Miami, you know that ho crazy! I don't even know why you tripping."

In a way he was right, people hated us being together, especially Kierra. But, after everything that has happened, it was easier to believe her over him because of his inconsistent ways these past couple of weeks.

He grabbed my hand "You know I care about you but, that's what happens when you get with a man like me, people are going to start stuff, get used to it. If you love me you wouldn't let anybody come between us."

Jamier had a way of making sense, he was well known and popular and I was lucky that he wanted me, but he was right certain things just came with the territory.

I calmed myself down and apologized to him about the way I was acting and leaned over and kissed him.

He turned up the radio and we drove over to his house. I wanted to let him know just how sorry I was so I performed oral sex on him, while he was driving. I loved making him happy and he was the best thing that ever happened to me. No matter what happened he knew I wasn't going anywhere, I was stuck like glue.

We pulled up to his house and he informed me that his parents were out of town for the weekend; he wanted me to stay the weekend with him. He scooped me out of the car and as soon as we got in the house, he laid me on the couch and we made love. I had to remind myself that I was lucky that he wanted me and if I wanted him to keep wanting me, I had to deal with whatever came our way and I was willing to deal. I would do anything for his love.

I woke up to the sound of something ringing, I noticed it was Jamier's house phone. Out of curiosity, I slid from under him hoping not to wake him, so I could answer the phone. The person hung up before I could answer and my nosiness led me to check the caller I.D.

Roberta Johnson
June 7, 2003 10:08a
803-678-4566

49

Johnson was Kierra's last name, and I wondered if that was her calling him. I decided to click back on the caller I.D. and all I saw was Roberta Johnson's number day after day, multiples time a day and at all hours of the night. That had to be Kierra's number. My stomach dropped and my hands started shaking, I decided to call the number back. I picked up the cordless phone and walked into the hall bathroom so Jamier wouldn't hear me.

"She just won't stop." I thought as I waited for someone to answer the phone.

"Hello." someone finally answered, it was an older voice maybe it was her mom.

"Ma, I got it." I hear Kierra say into the phone.

"Hello." Kierra said.

"You just won't stop, leave my man alone." I yelled into the phone.

"You silly little girl, Jamier can't leave me alone. You better chill out before you get your little feelings hurt." Kierra replied.

"You wish you could hurt my feelings." I shot back.

"Me and Jamier, still sleeping around, every time he claims to be with Des, he be with me. We have sex everywhere from his car, to my house even at his house, while you at work looking pitiful. He can't get enough of me, and he won't ever leave me alone. You're just something to do, he got caught up with you, but he knows what it is."

I was all confused. My emotions were all over the place. *"Is this the truth or is she lying?"* I thought to myself. I wanted to cry right then and there, but I couldn't let her know she had the best of me, so I replied the best way I knew how.

"Kierra, you're just jealous and you want to be me, leave him alone."

"Joy, I could be you, but I don't want to. I don't want the headache, so that's why I choose to just sleep around with him. I rain on your parade because you think you're something and your man don't even care about you like that; the way he be talking. Joy you'll find out sooner than later, go in his top drawer there's a red note book, your proof is right there and don't call me anymore little girl."

She hung up on me and I broke down in the bathroom. I was tired of this chick and I wanted to know what she was talking about, so I was determined to find this notebook. I crept back into his room, with tears falling from my face, relieved to see that he was still sleeping. I wondered what was inside this notebook.

I tiptoed over to the dresser and opened his top drawer and there it was *"The Red Notebook"*. My heart started racing again and I grabbed the notebook quickly and ran back to the bathroom, locking the door behind me. I sat down on the toilet and my heart sank.

Feb 20

Jamier,

Babe I'm so happy to have you back in my life, I would like to give us another try, but I don't know if you're ready. I got us this notebook to write back and forth while we're at school

Ke Ke

Ke Ke,

I like kicking it with you again, cause that sex is the bomb. You know you'll always be my girl, I want you bad, I do.

Jay

Jamier ,

Well if you want me bad, why are wasting time with Joy?
Why did you even get into a relationship with that little
girl?

Ke Ke

After you couldn't take it no more and left me for college
boy, I met Joy and she was a cool girl. I actually started
liking her and I got with her to make you jealous and now I
see that it worked.

Jay

Feb 21

Jamier,
Oh, you were trying to make me jealous? At least the girl
could have been cute. Haha ha-ha.

Ke Ke

The sad truth is I like you, but I do like her too but if you
just say the word, I can cut her off.

Jay

I was angry, and devastated. I just didn't know what to do. Jamier said he loved me and now I find out he just used me to make Kierra jealous. I flipped through a couple more pages.

4/30

Jamier,

Yo, I know I messed up and I slept around with Kevin. He must have given it to me. I didn't know, I had no clue. I had a great time with you in Miami and I felt like we could try to make us work.

Ke Ke

You said you were done with Kevin, so why you still messing around with him? Then you let that nigga burn you and I gave it to Joy, but you want us to make it work but you still messing with Kevin, cut him off and maybe I'll cut Joy off.

Jay

I guess we in the same boat. I've been waiting on you to let Joy go but, you still holding on to her. I'm tired of being on the side, make it right boo.

KeKe

Give me time. After this school year, I'll cut her off, I promise. I'll be over later, I know you miss it.

Jay

I read enough. My heart was torn into pieces, and my face was stained with tears. This man has been playing me and I felt sick to my stomach. I know I said I would deal with anything that came my way but I didn't know it would feel this painful. I tried to make sense of it all but I couldn't. I was pissed and like a pressure cooker, I was about to blow my lid.

I opened the bathroom door and when I stepped back into the room he was still sleeping. My anger got the best of me and I slapped him across the face with the notebook. He jumped up quick.

"Yo, what is wrong with you?" He yelled.

"You're a liar, you're a liar, you've been sleeping with Kierra the whole time and you let her burn you!" I screamed.

I slapped him again.

"Why are you doing this to me?" I yelled to the top of my lungs and then I started punching him one after another. I've never been so angry, he grabbed me and threw me on the bed.

"What the hell are you talking about?" he was still acting confused.

"I found your little red notebook, you liar, I hate you!" I screamed.

Anger filled his face.

"Yo, why are you going through my stuff?"

"Your little hoe told me to." I snapped back.

"Man, shut the up , shut up ." He yelled back.

"Just tell the truth." I screamed.

He climbed on top of me and pinned me down. We tussled a bit.

"Shut up and listen, Joy." He shouted.

"Yea, I was sleeping around with her and truthfully I was torn. I just wanted to get her out of my system and she's out now but I wasn't going to break up with you, I fed her some of that crap in that notebook just to keep sleeping with her."

   With every syllable that flowed from his lips, tears ran down my cheeks.

"Joy, you know how much I care about you, but you know I'm young also and with me being a star player it's hard to be faithful. I did have a few on the side but I never treated them like I treated you. They all knew about you and knew that I loved you. I want us to move on from here, I promise that you will always be my main girl."

All I could do was cry, and as much pain and betrayal I felt, sadly my heart won this round. Even after everything he has done, I chose to stay and love him, because when it's real love you don't let trivial things tear you apart, they were just side women and they will never have my spot. I was his Main Chick and I wasn't going anywhere.

We shared a kiss.

"Jamier, just promise, you'll never treat them like you treat me. Promise me things will get better soon."

"Baby, I promise."

Chapter 8

"Broken Promises"

"I guess promises are meant to be broken." I thought to myself as I sat in the passenger seat of Shantel's car as she drove me to the clinic for the third time this year. It's been about a year and a half, I had finally turned seventeen and we were just three months into the new year. I found myself at the clinic again behind Jamier. All the things he promised went out the window as soon as he went to college. It was woman after woman. I even caught him with one in his dorm last year. I fought for the number one spot in his life and I just didn't want to surrender my spot to another woman. I still wanted him, so I stayed.

Jamier and I have been through a lot over this past year and a half. Jamier was a star on his college basketball team and he wasn't going to let me or anybody get in the way of it, even when I told him I was pregnant with his child. He convinced me to abort the child, after threatening to break up with me if I didn't. His career came first and he didn't have time to be a father but he still wanted to have sex with me without condoms, even after I told him I could no longer take the pill because it was making me sick. He was aware of the risk of pregnancy but he didn't care, abortion was the solution to my pregnancy "problem".

After the first pregnancy, I ended up getting pregnant three more times and to the abortion clinic I went alone. I laid there and let them suction out not one, but three more babies, the babies I so desperately wanted. The babies I wanted to love. I am still not over it. It was a tough time in my life and my man Jamier never showed any sympathy, he just claimed it was for the best and convinced me to "suck it up". That whole situation messed me up but I didn't have the strength to stop having sex with him or to make him use condoms, so now he started using the pull-out method when we had sex, to ensure he wouldn't get me pregnant. Although he didn't get me pregnant, he gave me Chlamydia two times back to back last month.

Our relationship was falling apart and there were more bad times and bad arguments than there were good times. We literally argued about some other girl daily. I just didn't trust Jamier and all his other relationships with other women started to take a toll on me. I was growing tired of the drama, but I wanted to be his ride or die, so I decided to continue riding for him.

"Girl, I'm so dang on tired of coming up in this place, the nurse told me last time that I shouldn't come back to back like that but I'm tired of hurting." I said to Shantel.

"I know girl. It's a shame what we go through with these men, but that's love."

"Yea, but I'm just tired of coming up to this health department, maybe he'll get it together."

"Him and Des both, sometimes you just have to stick with them through the storm, it shall be over soon."

"I hope so. This last year has been hell, you know with me and the pregnancies, I'm just tired of crying, you know?"

"No one said love will be easy, Jamier will get it together, I promise" Shantel said.

"He better, because this is the last time I'm coming here." I said as we pulled into the parking lot of the health department.

■■

"Tie these balloons to that pink ribbon over there."

Ms. Ann said to me as we set up for Shantel's baby shower. It was mid-July and Shantel was seven months pregnant. She didn't even know until she was about four months. Desmond was no better than Jamier except he didn't push her to get an abortion, and that made her even more willing to stay with him, so they could be a family.

"Where do you want me to put the juices?" Shantel's Brother Micah asked Ms. Ann.

"Go sit them over there on the table and hurry up and go get the cups and ice, we're running out of time." Ms. Ann said as she was moving frantically to finish getting things together.

"Joy, go upstairs and check on Shan, and make sure she's dressed, everybody will be here soon." Ms. Ann commanded.

"Yes, Ma'am" I said as I ran upstairs to check on Shantel.

I walked in her room, she was twirling around in the mirror, staring at her belly and rubbing it. As much as I loved her, I had mixed emotions about the baby shower. I wanted to feel my babies, I wanted to be a mom. I started to cry, but then quickly caught myself trying not to ruin her day. She turned towards the door and saw me standing there.

"Hey, are you ready?" I asked.

"How do I look? I feel fat, Do I look fat?" She said waddling over to the door.

"Naw girl, stop it. You look pretty."

Even though she was pregnant she wore it well. She had on a long rose colored pink halter dress with a blue jean jacket cover up. She pulled her hair into a high bun and she had a few loose curls that fell into her face. She covered her lips with light pink lip gloss, she glowed. I almost teared up again.

"Joy are you, ok? Is all this ok for you?" She asked.

"Oh girl, I'm good. It's all good." I lied. I didn't want to ruin her day, so I pushed my feelings to the side so I could be there for her. "Your mom is waiting for you to come down, I'll let her know you're coming now."

She leaned over and hugged me.

"Thanks sis, I love you" she said.

"Love you too." I said as I turned away and walked down the stairs trying to compose myself.

Everyone started coming in. Her aunts, uncles and cousins and some of Desmond's family showed up as well. Every seat was taken. Then Desmond came in and tagging alongside of him was Jamier. My stomach was in Knots; I hadn't heard from Jamier in months. The last time we had a real conversation was when I saw him back in April. After that he stopped calling me; every time I called he was busy or not there, he grew a little distant but he never officially broke up with me so I held on. I had mixed feelings about seeing him. On one hand, I missed him so much but on the other hand, I couldn't stand him for the way he's been treating me lately.

Desmond walked in and spoke to everyone and kissed some of his family members and then took a seat next to Shantel.

Jamier made his rounds and then he finally made his way over to me, which I wish he hadn't done; I didn't want to go off on him in Ms. Ann's house. I walked away and went outside on the back deck and he followed behind.

"Hey Joy." he said flashing those pretty white teeth, those were my weakness, but I told myself to stay strong.

"Oh, now you know me?"

"Don't act like that." He said grabbing at my arm.

"Stop. Leave me alone, I'm busy." I said pulling my arm away from him.

"Busy doing what? You're supposed to always have time for me." he said grabbing at my arm again.

"Oh, really? So, I guess that applies to you as well." I shot back moving away from him towards the house.

"Why you are acting like that?" he asked.

"Why are you acting like that? I haven't heard from you in like 3 months. I thought I was your girl?"

"You know how it is in college. I have basketball practice and then I have my classes. When I'm done, I be tired."

"No, but I know how you are up at college, but you still could call me."

"My Bad. I'll do better, I promise. I miss you, he misses you too." he said pointing towards his pants.

He leaned in to kiss me. He was fine, and he had cut his braids, so that added to his sex appeal. I was like putty in his hands, and I couldn't help but kiss him back.

"You know you're the only girl I want."

"I am, huh" I laughed sarcastically.

"Man let's go to my car for a minute." He pulled me by the hand and I followed him to his car.

As much as I tried to stay strong. I caved in. He drove us over to the wooded area near Ms. Ann's house. He put the car in park and leaned over and started kissing me on my neck. I was well aware of what he wanted to do and without hesitation I allowed him to proceed. I missed him and I just wanted things to go back to what they use to be. We decided to get in the back seat of his car and we made love and it was mind blowing. I really missed him and I couldn't let him go if I tried. Jamier will always have my heart.

We got ourselves together and drove back to the baby shower. Before we snuck back in. Jamier promised that things would get better and surprisingly I believed him this time. My heart pushed me to stay.

Chapter 9

"Something Different"

"Girl, are you sure you can bowl, wobbling like that?" one of our co-workers asked Shantel.

"I'm going to try and maybe I will go into labor." Shantel replied.

It has been a week since her baby shower at Ms. Ann's house and because several co-workers couldn't make it, they all decided to get together at the bowling alley and throw her a shower there.

"She better sit down. I ain't trying to clean up no blood." I said Joking.

"Whatever." she said laughing as she went to sit down to put on her shoes, which I had to help her put on.

The bowling alley was packed, which is usual for a Saturday night and they were playing some nice music over the PA system. It looked like we were going to have some fun. I put on my bowling shoes and the game was on.

"Alright, Joy. It's your turn." Ms. Mary my manager said.

"Don't hate ya'll when I get this strike." I said to my co-workers talking a little friendly smack.

I walked up to the bowling lane and I could feel someone staring at me. I notice this heavyset guy looking at me, but I paid it no mind and kept bowling. Every time I went up to bowl, the guy was staring at me. He put me in the mind frame of Ice Cube, except he was light skin. He had on a Lakers Jersey and some blue Jeans. This time after I bowled my turn, I gave him a little smirk and went to sit down and he couldn't take his eyes off me.

"Do you know him?" Shantel whispered in my ear.

"Naw, girl and I don't know why he keep staring."

"Maybe, he wants you." she said in a whiny voice.

"You know I don't do chubby dudes and besides, I have a man."

"When the last time you heard from him?" she said cutting her eye at me.

"Shantel don't start, you know Jamier and I are good."

"I'm not saying to leave Jamier; maybe you can have a friend, ain't nothing wrong with friends."

"Yea, but I ain't that type of girl."

"Ya'll could just be friends, you ain't got to give him the cookie." She said laughing.

"Whatever, I got to go to the bathroom, bowl my turn." I said as I walked towards the bathroom.

As I walked out of the bathroom the Ice Cube look alike was standing right outside of the door. I walked right past him hoping he wouldn't stop me but he did.

"Hey, Beautiful." he said in a New York accent.

"Um, hey." I said a little irritated that he followed me to the bathroom.

"You're beautiful ma. Can I get to know more about you?"

"I can't. I got a man."

"I' ain't tryna get to know him. I want to get to know you. Plus, I know he ain't treating you right, let a real nigga take care of you."

"He does just fine." I responded defensively.

"If you don't mind me asking, how old are you Ma?"

"I'm seventeen, you?"

"I'm twenty-four. You're almost legal and I can work with that. Let me get your math?"

"My what?" I replied not understanding his New York lingo.

"Let me get your number. By the way I'm Rayshawn and you?"

"I'm Joy."

"You are a Joy, and you thick in all the right places."

He made me blush. Over the past two years, I've gained about forty pounds dealing with Jamier. Jamier said I was getting too big, but it was kind of his fault. Every time he would cheat I would binge eat to console the pain. Ain't nothing like Loaded Nachos when you're feeling sad and lonely. Jamier's cheating behavior took a toll on me and my self-esteem. I wasn't confident in my own skin, so it was nice to hear someone compliment me.

"See you're smiling, I bet your man don't make you smile, does he?"

"I mean, we're good." I said a little annoyed.

"Yea, ok. So, are you going to give me your number?"

I was a little reluctant at first, because I was still with Jamier, but what the heck, having a friend wouldn't hurt. I gave Rayshawn my number and he promised me he would call me the next day.
He asked for a hug and I gave him one and went on back to the game. He said he wanted to show me something different, something I ain't never seen before. I was curious to see what it was.

• •

"Get whatever you want." Rayshawn said to me while we shopped at *BEBE* at the mall.

"I told you I wanted to show you something different and take care of you, whatever you want it's all yours."

"Really, Rayshawn? Thank you" I said with excitement giving him a hug to show how thankful I was.

It's been about two months since I've met Rayshawn. Jamier and I never officially broke up, he stopped calling and after begging and begging him to make what we had work, he finally confessed that he wanted to move on. He was tired of the drama with me as if he wasn't the cause of all the drama. I was really hurt about it, I latched on to Rayshawn and Jamier became an afterthought.

Rayshawn was something different; something
I've never had. He had money and plenty of it and
from the first time we hung out, he spent it on me. He
took me to the finest restaurants and shopping to the
most expensive stores. He was very secretive about
how he made his money and I didn't bother
questioning him if he was spending it on me.

He knew how to treat a girl and made me feel
comfortable every time we hung out. We started
having sex a couple of weeks after we met, and
although he was nothing like Jamier, I knew he liked
me and he treated me good, so I made myself deal
with it.

"I want to give you what you never had, show you
places you never seen. I want you to do things you've
never done, but I need you to trust me." he said.

"Oh, I trust you." I said looking confused.

"I need to know you're down for me and you're never
going anywhere."

"Why would I? look what you're doing for me? I ain't
never had a guy treat me like this."

"I got us a room tonight at the *Hilton*. So, Ima take
you to *Victoria Secret* and I want you to pick out
something sexy to wear tonight."

"What are you up to?" I asked.

"It's a surprise, you'll see."

My face lit up. Rayshawn was growing on me by the day. He knew how to make me smile and make me feel good and a girl like me needed this is my life.

We finished up my shopping and he dropped me back off at Ms. Ann's.

He said he was going to be back at 9:30pm to pick me up and he wanted me to wear the lingerie he bought for me earlier. As soon as I got in the house, I gave Shantel the scoop about today and she was so happy for me. After talking to her, I jumped in the shower to prepare for tonight. I couldn't help but wonder what my surprise was.

When I got out of the shower, I grabbed my *Victoria Secret Amber Romance* lotion and applied it over my body. I made sure to put on the lingerie, and it was the Middle of September and the weather was still warm so I decided to wear a sleeveless black *BEBE* dress I copped at the mall earlier. It hugged my curves nicely. I decided to flat iron my hair which fell a little pass my shoulders. I applied some lip-gloss to my lips and I was ready to go. *"I hope Rayshawn like it."* I thought to myself.

Rayshawn pulled up a little earlier than 9:30. I rushed out the house with my overnight bag and hopped into his all black 2004 *Mercedes S500*. He sped off and we flew down the highway towards the hotel. After a little small talk, we finally arrived at the hotel.

"I have a reservation for Rayshawn Smith." Rayshawn told the hotel clerk.

"Did you want a smoking or non-smoking room?"
she asked.

"Give us smoking." he replied.

I examined the hotel as Rayshawn was finishing up
with the hotel clerk. The hotel was nice and I couldn't
believe I was here. Rayshawn was such a great guy,
he made me happy and I could see us falling in love.

"You ready?" Rayshawn said to me interrupting my
thoughts.

We walked into the elevator.

"Where is our room?" I inquired.

"We on the top floor baby, Penthouse baby!"

"Really? You got us the Penthouse? I bet that cost a
lot?"

"It's nothing, really. I want you to get used to living
like this."

I leaned over and kissed him.

"I appreciate you. Thank you, babe, is this my
surprise?"

"Yea, part of it."

We finally arrived at our floor, we got off the elevator and we made our way to our room. When Rayshawn opened the door, I was blown away. The suite was amazing. I felt like I was in a dream and I couldn't believe all of this was for me.
 Rayshawn told me to look around because he needed to step outside on the balcony to make a phone call. Everything was nice from the bathroom to the bedroom.

 "I could live like this forever." I thought to myself, as I placed my bag in the closet in the bedroom.

"While you're in their Joy, go ahead and take that dress off." Rayshawn yelled to me while I was in the bedroom.

I slid the dress off and made my way back into the living room area. I see Rayshawn rolling a blunt and he had a bottle of Grey Goose sitting on the table next to his weed and a bag full of pills. I sat down next to him and waited for him to finish rolling the blunt.

"You so thick ma." he said as he lit the blunt.

   He took a hit and then passed it to me. I picked back up my weed habit when I started dealing with Rayshawn; he smoked, so I smoked with him. We smoked until the blunt became a short and then he passed me a shot of liquor and told me to chug it down.

He then passed me three more shots, I tossed them back and then I heard a knock on the door. Rayshawn got up and opened the door and it was his homeboy Mello at the door. I was wondering what he was doing here, Rayshawn let him in.

"What's happening, Joy?" Mello asked.

"Nothing, Nothing, chilling." I responded. I was high and the liquor was starting to get to me. Mello came and sat in the chair next to me and Rayshawn. Rayshawn passed the bottle of Grey Goose to Mello and he chugged it straight from the bottle. Mello began making small talk with Rayshawn and all sudden I felt Rayshawn hand on my thigh. He then started moving it up my thigh and he found his way to my vagina.

"Rayshawn, what are you doing, Mello is right there" I whispered to him.

"Chill out. That's my boy, he cool, it's all good." He said.

I didn't know what was going on, but I had no other reason not to trust him.

I let him continue.

Rayshawn started moving his fingers around my inside of me. The next thing I know, Mello stood up and walked over to me and his penis was hanging out of his pants.

"Yo, what the heck?" I said to Rayshawn.

"Joy, chill. That's my homeboy and I told him, how special you were to me. He wanted to come see about you himself, he's more like my brother. So, if you like me, you'll like him; Let's have some fun tonight. You said you want to try something different."

"Fun like what?" I asked.

"I want you to let me and my homie smash." He said.

"But, why would I do that?" I said with my face screwed up.

He leaned in and kissed me right on the lips and then he said,

"You my girl, right? you said you want to see me happy and well this will make me happy."

I got stuck at the "my girl" part and this was the first time he's ever referred to me as that. He must have really liked me and he was right. I wanted to make him happy; he treated me so well and what would it really hurt when no one has to know. My hesitation slowly faded away.

Rayshawn asked me to climb into his lap, my back facing him and we began having sex, then Mello came closer and asked me for oral sex and I obliged him. I couldn't believe I was doing this, I was having sex with two men at the same time.

After about an hour of them taking turns with me, Mello ended up leaving and Rayshawn and I laid in the bed.

"So, I'm your girl?" I asked.

"Yes, you're my down chick. I know you will hold me down. I told you, you're something special"

I smiled and Rayshawn was truly something different. He was exposing me to things I've never seen, and now that I'm his girl, I'm willing to do anything to keep him wanting me.

Chapter 10

"Do it For Daddy"

I woke up to the sound of something buzzing; I notice my cellphone vibrating on the night stand next to my bed. I rolled over and reached for my phone and realized it was 12:40 pm; I was supposed to be at work at 2pm. I also noticed I had 6 missed calls from Rayshawn.

I've been dealing with Rayshawn now for the past six months and I was two and a half months away from graduating from high school; something Ms. Ann was happy about. Rayshawn continued to be the guy that I met and I hadn't had any issues with other women since I started dealing with him. He threw money at me whenever I needed it, but I still worked at Taco Bell. I didn't want Ms. Ann to ever get suspicious about the things I was obtaining from him.

Rayshawn introduced me to some crazy stuff, especially when it came to sex. We tried threesomes together with other men and women. We would go to strip clubs together and pay for VIP; the stripper would perform oral sex on him and me.We did anal, he wanted me to spank him and the list goes on. He opened a new world for me; It was wild and crazy, but he always made sure to protect himself,so we had no issues with STD's or Pregnancies. Rayshawn was my man and there was nothing I wouldn't do for him; I was falling in love.

I picked up my cellphone and decided to call Rayshawn back.

"Yo, what are you doing?" he said into the phone.

"Hey babe. My bad. I was sleep, what's up?" I said.

"What you got going on today?"

"I'm supposed to go to work at two."

"When you going to quit that job, and let me show you how to make real money?"

"When you can show me how to make real money" I shot back.

"Aight, bet. Call out today, matter of fact let them know you're quitting today. I want to take you somewhere."

"I can't just quit on them, like that."

"You would if you want to make this real money, would I ever steer you wrong?"

"No, you wouldn't. Ok, well let me call you back."

We hung up the phone.

I had been working at *Taco Bell* for about three and a half years and I couldn't believe that today was going to be my last day. Rayshawn was right, I needed to be making real money. He had exposed me to places and things I would have never seen, if it wasn't for the type of money he had. I knew in my heart; I would never get those things for myself if I stayed working at *Taco Bell.* I like what Money could afford me and I didn't want to miss this opportunity.

It was about 8:30pm and Rayshawn was on his way to Ms. Ann's house to pick me up. He said he was taking me to his business partner's house and that I needed to dress nice. I settled on a Blue Jean *Baby Phat* dress, that came a little above the knee. I paired it with my black *Gucci* flip flops, pulled my hair into a side ponytail, threw on some silver hoop earrings and put some lip-gloss on my lips. I still had some weight on me, and although Rayshawn never said much about it, I still didn't feel pretty, I hated my body. I gave myself another look over in the mirror until I was satisfied. I splashed some of my *Victoria Secret Love Spell* across my skin, as I dashed out the door.

We drove to the outskirts of the city to a housing development. The homes were beautiful, homes you see on TV and in the magazine. We finally pulled up to a brick two story home. As soon as we pulled up, I noticed a black Jaguar and a black Range Rover parked in the drive way.

"His business partner living good." I thought to myself.

We made our way out of the car and walked up to the door. Rayshawn rang the doorbell and a beautiful woman opened the door. She was brown skin, medium height and her body was nice. She had average size breast, a thin waist and wide hips; She had the perfect shape. She was dressed in a pink tank top and blue jean capris. She kind of favorited Tatiana Ali from *Fresh Prince of Bel-Air*; she was gorgeous. I started to feel a little intimidated.

"Hey, Sis." Rayshawn said and he leaned in to hug and kiss her.

"Sis." I thought to myself. I thought we was going to meet his business partner.

"Joy, this is my sister Chocolate." Rayshawn said.

"Nice to meet you." I said as I extended my hand to shake hers.

"Nice to meet you too. Rayshawn has told me a lot about you" She said giving me a smirk. "Come on in ya'll, let me make ya'll a drink"

We walked into her home and it was beautiful. She had two living rooms and they were both decorated with all white furniture. As we made our way through her house to her back office, I noticed she had a lot of pictures of herself hanging around the house. Her office was huge, she had a white loveseat in her office and a desk with a desk chair.

I made myself comfortable on the love seat and Rayshawn sat next to me. Chocolate finally made her way back to the office, handed Rayshawn and I a drink and took her seat in the chair behind the desk. She jumped right to the point.

"So, Joy. Ray told me you're interested in making some real money." Chocolate inquired.

"Yea, I am."

"I just need to make sure you're really down for what we do."

"Yes, I'm down. I want to live like you." I said laughing a bit looking around her house.

"Ok, take off your dress."

"Huh? What you mean?"

I looked over at Rayshawn and he gave me that look, like I should do what she says. Rayshawn and I have done some freaky stuff, but I was unsure about this.

"Can you take your dress off? I want to see what you're working with under that dress. Ray is she down or is she going to keep asking all these questions?"

Ray looked at me and then he said, "Can you take your dress off for daddy?"

I didn't know what was going on, but I did trust Rayshawn. I knew he would never put me in any situation that would hurt me. I nervously stood up and started to slowly unbutton my dress until it was finally resting on the floor. There I stood in my bra and panties not knowing what to expect next.

"Rayshawn, she's thick. She's going to have to tighten up that stomach; we could work on that." Chocolate said.

"There's one more thing I need to see, can you dance? Ima turn on this music and I want you to dance like you do at a party." She said to me.

I've never been put on the spot like this before to dance in front of two people. My nerves started to get the best of me, butterflies lingered in the pit of my stomach and my palms started to sweat. I wanted to run out of there, but on the other hand I wanted to show Rayshawn that I was ready to make real money. I paused for a second and even though the music was playing I couldn't move, my nerves got the best of me.

"Yo, Ray. You sure she down?" Chocolate asked.

"Yea, let me holla at her."

Rayshawn approached me and whispered in my ear.

"You're mine, right? I want to see you have everything you never had. So, I need you to do this. Trust me! Do it for Daddy."

He handed me a drink and I swallowed it quickly. I was still nervous, but I wanted to impress Rayshawn. I needed to show him that I was down for him. She started the music over and it was an Oldie, but Goodie. *Ying Yang Twins "Whistle while you Twerk"* came blasting through the speakers. I put my hands on my knees and I started bouncing my booty. I began to dance as if no one was watching me. By the looks on their faces, I could tell that they were happy with my little performance.

"O.K. good, Joy. Go ahead and get dressed and we'll be back." Chocolate said.

Chocolate and Rayshawn walked out of the office, to some other part of the house. I put my dress back on and sat back down on the couch trying to catch my breath.

"Rayshawn was forever having me do some crazy things." I thought to myself.

They finally came back into the office and Rayshawn sat in the chair behind the desk; Chocolate sat next to me on the loveseat.

"Joy, I brought you over here, so I can introduce you to the kind of work I do. We needed to see if you were a good fit for us; Chocolate and I own a local Strip Club. Chocolate is the Big Sister to all the strippers and she'll be the one taking care of you, helping you with anything you need. You will work Thursday through Sunday and we'll discuss the hours later. This is how you get to make real money at my club. You'll make more in one night than you would for a month at *Taco Bell*. All the money you make isn't directly all yours. I get 30%, Chocolate gets 20% of your tips and you always cash out at night. Your stage name will be Joy, we like it. If Chocolate feels like you need another name, we'll change it later. Tomorrow I'm going to have Chocolate get with you so she can help you with routines, your hair and stuff. Is this something you think you can do?"

"Yeah." I said in agreeance, but deep down I was unsure about the stripping thing.

We discussed a few other things and we finally said our Goodbyes; Rayshawn and I went on our way. On the car ride home, all I could think about was the stripping, and I wondered why he never mentioned the club to me. My thoughts were interrupted as Rayshawn told me to get out of the car; I noticed we were at his condo. We walk inside of his house and I found myself a space on his couch. He went into his kitchen and came back with two shots of liquor; We toasted to "More Money". He took a seat right next to me on the couch.

"You're special Joy, and I knew the first day I met you that you would be my down chick."

I blushed. "But why didn't you tell me you owned a strip club?"

"The timing wasn't right, and I wanted to get to know you. I wanted you to know me before really finding out what I do."

"I'm your girl though, why do you want me to strip?"

"Who better than my girl, I need you to help me make this money.

"This is all new to me. I've never done anything like this; I'm a little scared."

"You got this, Joy. You're so sexy and you're thick as hell. Men will pay good money to see you."

"You're sure about that?" I said questioning what he saw in me.

"You, remember my boy Mello? He talks about you all the time; how sexy you are and I know if he thinks that way, other men would kill to have a piece of you. When I first met you, that's what drew me in, your sexy body. I envisioned myself in between your thighs and if any other men are like me, they would have that same vision. The money would be pouring in and think about what you could do with all that money."

He leaned over, kissed me and pushed me back onto the couch. He reached his hand up my dress, pulled off my underwear, climbed on top of me and we made love.

"I'm trusting you. I'm still a little nervous" I whispered in his ear.

He whispered back "I got you. If you don't do it for anyone else, at least do it for Daddy."

There was something about Rayshawn that made me feel at ease, even though I never ever thought about stripping, I knew Rayshawn would have my back. I decided to give it a try; what could it hurt? I wanted the money and I wanted to live a good life with Rayshawn. I kissed him on his neck and we made love into the wee hours of the morning.

Chapter 11

"Rayshawn's Game"

It was a beautiful Summer day in August and Shantel and I agreed to meet each other at a local eatery to grab a bite to eat. It's been about two months since I've hung out with Shantel since she moved out of Ms. Ann's house. After graduation, Shantel and Desmond moved into an apartment together. I barely saw my sister; we both had a lot going on in our lives so it was nice to catch up with her.

I arrived at the place a little earlier than she did and grabbed us a table; I order a round of water for us. She came in about 10 minutes late. Shantel looked tired as she came through the door pushing a baby stroller. She had her hair pulled up in a high ponytail and she had on blue jeans shorts and a yellow tank top. Shantel was always a slim girl. She never had much breast or butt, she did put on a little weight during her pregnancy but I could tell it was coming off.

"Hey boo! What's up?" She said as we exchanged hugs.

"I miss ya'll, how are you doing?" I said as I bent down to kiss her daughter Aaliyah.

"She starting to look more and more like her daddy." I said as I sat down in my seat.

Shantel pulled her chair out and sat down.

"Girl, tell me about it and she act just like him, stubborn as a bull." she laughed.

"She's a good baby though. I haven't seen much of you lately, Rayshawn sure has you on lock." she gave me the side eye.

"Oh, whatever chick. Don't act like Desmond don't have you on house arrest. You probably got to be home in about ten minutes."

We shared a laugh.

"Girl, I'm still dealing with Des and his drama. I caught him again with Bianca, and this chick say she supposedly pregnant by Des, but she's lying. You know she's just jealous; she wants to be me. Besides his drama, I just be at the house, me and Aaliyah. I thought she would change him, but she ain't make no difference. He still be running the streets."

"Ugh, I never liked Bianca. She always running behind somebody man and all she does is lie. She gets on my nerves. She doesn't know who the daddy is, all the men she been with. Girl don't sweat it. She just love being the other woman, he knows what it is."

"Right. I told her just because I'm a mother that don't mean she won't get her face smashed in. I told Des he better stop playing with me before she gets hurt. I was going to call up to her job and try to get her fired."

"Girl, do it. I can't stand a side chick. Then maybe she'll leave him alone." I laughed.

"Right, she'll be jobless and man less but enough about me. So, how is the stripping going? I can't believe you stripping, you are a trip."

"I mean it's cool. I'm making more money than I ever would have if I was still at Taco Bell, but it's nothing like I thought it would be. Ray and I been having little issues since I started dancing, with the money and how he's been acting distant. It's a whole other world girl. "

When I initially started dancing, I would dance at night and then go to school during the day. I was exhausted, and because Ms. Ann worked nights she had no clue what was going on. I managed to graduate from high school and instead of college, I decided to stick with stripping; Dancing was a world of its own. I hadn't seen nothing like it; Men were hungry and they would pay anything to feed their fantasies.

Chocolate was cool and I never crossed her or got on her bad side. Before we would dance she would make a lot of us pop half of an ecstasy pill, we would smoke a blunt and throw back a couple of shots of liquor. She wanted us to let go of all our inhabitations.

Every night I worked, I made at least five hundred dollars and on some nights, I'll make close to a thousand. There were some girls, who had the stage on lock and they were cashing out two G's a night or more. When I would cash out at the end of the night, Rayshawn wouldn't be happy with me because I wasn't pulling in what he thought I should. So, he told Chocolate to tell me to start offering VIP to more of the men and he wanted me to do more than dance in the VIP room. At Ray's club, he let a lot go down in the VIP rooms that shouldn't normally go down and some girls had sex in the VIP room.

I had sex twice in the VIP room with a couple of men and got about five hundred a piece from them. Rayshawn wanted me to keep doing it, but after those two times I never had sex again in VIP; I couldn't bring myself to do it. I would let them touch on my vagina, play with my breast, suck on them and I'll play with their penises, but that was as far as I was going to go. Rayshawn was pissed off at me on the regular because I stopped having sex in VIP. I wanted to make money just like he did, but some of those men I just couldn't have sex with. The more I dance for Ray, the less he treated me like his girl and more like an employee. We still had sex from time to time, but it was nothing like it was before; Ray had changed.

Besides the drama with Ray, there was always some drama with the girls at the club. When I first started dancing, there were a couple of girls that hated seeing me with Ray because they use to be his girls. Word around the club was for me not to get comfortable, because there was only a matter of time before Ray would bring in a new girl to take my spot. "Speaking of the devil, ain't that Rayshawn walking in." she said pointing towards the door.

Yes, it was his fat self-coming through the door and he wasn't alone. He walked in with a young girl, she was light skin and had her hair in a bob cut. She did have a nice shape. She had on a short sleeve BabyPhat shirt and a pair of BabyPhat capris. She wasn't that pretty though.

"Oh, naw Shan! I'm about to flip. Who the heck is she? Cause he most definitely was in my bed last night."

"Joy, calm down. Now you know out of all people, I would be pissed too. Maybe she's trying to get a job as a stripper or a waitress at the club. Maybe it's not what it seems."

"Hey, Joy. What's up Ma?" he said as he approached my table.

I gave him the finger and rolled my eyes.

He laughed. "See ya tonight."

He turned around and walked over to his table and little Miss BabyPhat followed behind.

"No, he did not! No, he did not, Shan! "

My blood was boiling. Last night he was laid in my bed kissing all over me and now he up in this restaurant with some chick. We ain't never had any problems with other women and I hope it wasn't about to start now. Although we've been having issues lately, and he hasn't been treating me the best, he was still my man. Little Miss Baby Phat wasn't about to take what was mine.

"Joy, I really think he's interviewing her. Do you think he would really bring another chick in your face?"

"I'm sure, he didn't expect to see me here."

"Yea, but he also came over and spoke to you. Give him a break, if he was cheating, he probably would have tried to dodge you."

"Yea, maybe, we never had any issue with other girls so maybe he is interviewing her for a job at the club, we shall see." I said cutting my eye over in his direction as we walked out of the place.

I hoped Shantel was right about Rayshawn and little Miss BabyPhat was just looking for a job. I didn't want to lose Rayshawn. I was in love with him and I don't know what I would do if he called it quits.

∙∙

Sure, enough Little Miss Baby Phat was my replacement. He flaunted her around the club like he did me and I was pushed to the side. He treated me like a stranger.

The more he ignored me the more I tried to get his attention. I could tell he didn't feel the same about me and I still gave him sex whenever he asked. Although it was awful, I knew that was the only way I could spend time with him. I couldn't understand how he could just detach himself from me and as much as I hate to admit it those other girls were right, it was only a matter of time.

"I can't believe he would do that to me." I said to my girl Cyn, as I was getting dressed to do my set.

I wasn't cool with many of the girls at the club because of Ray, but there was this one girl name Cyn, who took me under her wing. She was very sweet and she didn't seem like the type that would strip. She was mixed with Hawaiian and Black, very pretty. She's favored Ashanti and her body was a gift from God. She had the perfect everything and she made good money. She was one of the pros and we started hanging hard outside of the club. Getting high and making side money dancing for men outside of the club; The men loved her. We would make good money together, which we didn't have to give to Rayshawn.

"Girl, believe it! That's his game. He finds ya'll little young girls and turn ya'll out. He flashes money in ya'll face and he makes ya'll fall in love with him, so he can use ya'll to make money for him in this club."

"Naw, it wasn't like that. Me and Ray had a good thing going on."

"Yea, that's what Shai, Mickey, Ashley, Destiny and the other ones thought until he played them too. That's what he does, he preys on the weak. See I went to school with Chocolate, that's how I started stripping, but he tried to run that game on me and I wasn't having it. He knew better than to play that with me."

"But, what am I supposed to do now? I love him."

"Girl, what did I tell you about Love? You don't love no nigga, only this paper. Get your money and forget about Ray; let him be her problem."

Chocolate interrupted Cyn and I.

"Yo, Joy. Ray wants to see you in his office right now" Chocolate said.

"Well, I'm about to go on and perform my set."

"We'll let Shai go on, he wants to see you right now."

"What does he want?" I asked acting irritated, rolling my eyes so Chocolate could see.

"I don't know, he just told me to come down and get you."

"Ugh, ok! I'm going." I slipped a dress over my stage outfit and made my way to his office. Even though I acted like his request bothered me, deep down I was excited about seeing him. I wondered what he wanted, maybe he wanted to get back together. So many thoughts ran through my head. I knocked on his door lightly.

"Come in!" I heard him yell from the other side of the door.

I walked in and to my surprise I was nervous.

"Close the door." he said.

I walked over and sat down in a chair directly across from him.

"How my little Joy doing?"

"I'm fine, but Ray how could you do me like this? You said I could trust you, but you played me with Nicki, and you bring her all up in my face."

"Joy, you were a cool girl and I liked you, but I have to run my business. What we had can go no further than what it was."

"So why did you say? I was your girl and you care and all that? Were you just running game?"

"What we had was cool, but like I said, you have to just understand that; That's over now. I put you in the position to make money, the money you said you wanted to make. Why you tripping over love?"

I could feel the tears swelling up in my eyes.

"So, was it real or were you running game?"

"Life is a game. Some of us play it and some of us get played. You must figure out which end you're on, but you wanted more then what I wanted . You got too clingy and all I was looking for was some fun."

"But you the one who said I was your girl first, you said that." I said elevated my voice.

"Joy, calm down. My bad if I hurt you, but you have to move on."

I rolled my eyes at him as I tried to fight back the tears.

"But, I didn't really bring you up here to talk about that, I have a favor, I want to ask you. I have a couple of my celebrity friends coming to the club and I want you, Cyn, Shai and Raven to dance for them. They're tipping big so make it worth their while. I also have another proposition for you and for you only. They want to have a little more fun after the club and it's about three of them. They're willing to pay fifteen hundred a piece for sex with you.

I'm only asking you because I know you'll do anything for me. I know you couldn't have sex with the men in VIP, but these dudes are my homies. They aren't bad looking dudes and I know them, so you should be good. This is good money and this could get you that car you've been saving for."

He stood up from his chair and walked over to me and rubbed his hand on my thigh.

"You think you could do it for me?"

Even after everything he did to me, a part of me still wanted him to want me, so I agreed to do it.

"Now Chocolate is going to set everything up and give the info to you. You won't be able to keep all the money, from this I need you to give me fifty percent and the rest would be yours, ok?"

"O.K." I replied.

"Before you leave, come put this in your mouth?" he said as he grabbed at his pants.

Without hesitation, I performed oral sex on Ray, even though I knew he doesn't feel the same about me; I can't shake him. I love Ray and I was still willing to do anything for him, just in hopes that maybe he'll want me back.

After we danced for Ray's celebrity friends. Chocolate drove me over to the hotel where the men were staying. She went over the plan with me, gave me their room number and the extra hotel key to let myself in. She also gave me another hotel key, for the room I'll be staying in after it was all done.
Before getting out of the car, I took three shots of liquor and took half of a pill. I told myself I wasn't going to have sex for money again since those times in the VIP room, but somehow, I let Rayshawn talk me into this. I grabbed my bag and got out of the car. Chocolate said she would wait outside for me until I let her know everything was good to go.
I walked into the hotel, my heart was beating fast from the elevator to the room door. My hands were shaking as I slid the key into the door. I walked in and there were three men sitting on the bed apparently waiting on me. The shortest one motioned for me to come over and sit on the bed next to him. No one said any words, we got straight down to business. The brown skin one came over and started undressing me.

He pulled my dress over my head and then he unsnapped my bra. He then pushed me back on the bed and pulled my panties down; out the corner of my eye I could see the tall one undressing as well. Everything became a blur, they had their way with me until the sun came up.

When I finally came to, I realized I was still in the hotel with all of them and laid across the bed naked. They were all asleep. I got up and I saw the money laying on the nightstand.I grabbed the money, my dress, under clothes, my bag and caught the elevator to my room.

I looked at my phone and noticed I had five missed calls and voicemails from Chocolate and two missed calls from Rayshawn. I didn't bother to respond.

I slid the key through the door to open it and I raced to the shower. I washed and washed and washed; I tried to scrub off every bit of last night. I was numbed and I felt dead on the inside. I cried, and cried; I sobbed profusely. I fell to the shower floor and lost myself in my tears. All this for Rayshawn, all of this for him and to think, all this was a game to him. I finally gathered myself together just enough to get up out of the shower. I laid my damp body across the bed, covered myself up with the blanket and cried myself to sleep.

Chapter 12

"Out with Old, In with the New"

"Put ya'll glasses in the air, give it up for our girl Joy, Happy birthday Joy!" The D.J said over the microphone.

"Thank you." I whispered to the D.J and to the other people around me.

Chocolate decided to throw me a party at the club to celebrate my eighteenth birthday. She gave me the day off, got me a booth and a couple of bottles. It was a surprise, and I was happy she did something for me because Rayshawn and I was at odds.

After the incident with the men, Rayshawn cheated me out of my money. He was supposed to get fifty percent and I was supposed to get the other fifty. Once I gave him the money, he kept seventy for himself and he gave Chocolate ten percent and left me with twenty. I was pissed off, but he tried to say he never agreed to give me fifty. The crazy thing about it, there was no way to prove him otherwise; I knew in the end he would win. I didn't bother trying to get what was due to me.

I started messing with his money; I would lie about how many tips I got, before cashing out.

I would give Cyn some of my tips to stash away. The longer I danced for Ray, the more he showed me how much he didn't like me. I saw a side of him, I never thought existed; He treated me like yesterday's trash. There would be times he would call me up to his office, we would have sex, and then he would throw me out. He was heartless and he didn't care about any of the feelings I had. I guess I was old news and Rayshawn wanted something new.

"Happy Birthday, Joy." Brian said tapping me on my shoulder.

I turned around, "Oh, thank you, Brian." I said.

He leaned in and whispered in my ear "You going to dance for me tonight?"

"Oh baby, I'm not dancing tonight."

"Can I talk to you?" he asked.

"Sure, that's cool. Come around here." I motioned for him to sit next to me in the booth.

Brian was a regular at the club and he often came to see me. He was a real cool dude and we became friends. He was very attractive; His skin was the color of dark chocolate. He was tall about five feet eleven and he favored Morris Chestnut. He was a lot older than me, but I could relate to him.

"Let me take you out of here." He said.

"And take me where, Brian?" I inquired.

"Up out of here. You know you don't want to be here."

"It's cool." I said.

"Yeah, but it ain't for you. How long you've been doing this anyway?"

"About six or seven months, something like that."

"I like you, Joy. You know I do. That's why I always come up here to see you. You're real sexy, and thick in all the right places."

I started blushing. "Brian, don't start. You and these men are all the same. Ya'll all run the same game, you ain't the only one trying to take me up out of here."

"But, I'm the only real one. I want to love you though, I want to be with you."

"You want to love me, really Brian?"

"Yea, Joy. I want to love you, I already care about you."

"I don't know, Brian. I'm tired of getting my heartbroken."

"I won't ever break your heart; just give me a chance. I really like you, let me take you out on one date."

"I'll think about it."

Brian wasn't saying anything I hadn't heard before. That's how a lot of these men talked when they came up in here. They wanted to love me and make me their girl. It's hard to tell if Brian was being truthful or just running the same game, but Brian did come here faithfully every week and he showed me the attention I was no longer getting from Rayshawn. He made me feel good, he wanted me and I desperately wanted someone to love me. I decided to take him up on his offer, to take me out on a date. For a girl that didn't have nothing to offer anyone, it felt good to be wanted by a man.

• •

I used the money I made at the club and I moved into a nice one bedroom apartment on a nice part of town. I bought a car with cash, a 1998 *Mercedes Benz* 325i. I was excited for my first date with Brian. Two weeks ago, at the club we exchanged numbers and we've been talking on the phone ever since. I was glad to finally make time to see him outside of the club; He was growing on me and I liked that.

I danced around my apartment to *50 Cent's "Candy Shop."* It was the beginning of November and the weather was getting cool. I wanted to be comfortable on our first date, so I put on a burgundy *Juicy Couture* Velour sweat suit and my black *UGG* boats.

I pulled my hair back into a low ponytail, threw on some lip gloss, grabbed my keys and hopped in my car to meet Brian at a local ice cream Shoppe.

Brian didn't dress as flashy as Rayshawn. He had on pair of dark blue jeans, a red Polo shirt and a black pair of Timberland boats; He looked nice. We ordered our ice cream and found us a little table in the corner; our conversations flowed.

Brian was thirty-two, single with no children. He grew up in a single parent home and he had five siblings; he was the youngest of them all. He never knew his father and his mother died from cancer when he was about 18. After his mother's death, him and his siblings lost touch. He was an Operational Manager at a local call center. He goes on to share his pain from previous relationships and how women used him and took advantage of him. He was just tired and wanted something genuine and he noticed that with me. I told him about Rayshawn, the club, about some of my other ex's and all the games they played. He reassured me that he wasn't going to hurt me or play games like they did. We had a lot of things in common especially our mother's deaths and our common heartbreaks. Neither one of us wanted to get hurt again and we both were ready for something real. Rayshawn was the old, Brian was the new and I was ready for the New.

Chapter 13

"He Has his Ways"

"Babe, call me when you get this message." This was the third message I left on Brian's phone. It was a little after ten and he said he would be home no later than eight. Today was our six-month anniversary and I had a wonderful evening planned for him and I. I started off by making his favorite meal, baked chicken smothered in gravy, rice and green beans with a piece of cornbread on the side.

Brian was a country boy and he loved some rice and gravy. I had the table set perfectly, glasses filled with soda. I wanted wine, but Brian was a recovering alcoholic and he was 1 year sober; I didn't want him going back. I also lit a few candles and scattered them around the table. Even though I lost a lot of weight dancing at the club, I was still uncomfortable with my body, but I wanted to step outside the box for him. I put on a black lace negligee, trying to get away from the t-shirt I always wore during our intimate times.

I peeked outside the window and Brian still was nowhere to be found. I started to get worried, and my insecurities got the best of me. Brian was a stickler for time and being late was out of the ordinary for him.

Over these pasts few months, Brian never gave me a reason to be insecure, but I couldn't help it. I never knew a man not to cheat, so I figured it was only a matter of time. So, when he acted out of the ordinary, I assumed he was cheating.

Brian and I became official last December, and a few weeks later he asked me to move in with him. I had never lived with a man, but things with Brian just felt right. We were good friends and we just clicked. As soon as he asked me to move in, I stopped dancing and I subleased my apartment to one of the girls from the club. Brian didn't want me to work, he said he'd take care of me, but I had about three thousand dollars saved from the club, that he wasn't aware of. Brian rented a townhome, in a decent part of Columbia, not where I would have preferred to stay but, it made due.

Brian was a very organized guy and I learned that quickly when I moved in with him. *"There was a place for everything and everything has a place."* he would often say. The house had to stay spotless. I remember this one time, I left maybe a bowl and/or spoon in the sink and then I went to bed. He woke me out of my sleep to wash those dishes. That probably led to one of our first big arguments and my first time seeing Brian's temper. To me those dishes could have been washed in the morning but to him, the kitchen isn't clean if there are dishes left in the sink. He said the least I could do is keep the house clean because he works and he did have a point. After that, I made sure to clean the house the way Brian liked it.

Brian was very funny about me leaving the house without him, and he was also particular about my friends. He didn't like a lot of people over his house either.

One time he came home and Shantel and Aaliyah were visiting. We were just watching TV and talking, we weren't doing anything out of the ordinary, but it was just the fact that he doesn't want anyone in the house, when he's not there. That led to another big argument which revealed Brian's anger problem. I made sure never to bring anyone to the house again.

Brian worked hard, and always took advantage of the overtime his job offered. He worked so much we barely hung out. Over these pasts few months our dates consisted of movies and our couch, so I was ready to spend some time with him tonight. I liked living with him; besides the little small stuff that aggravated me, he was my friend. I opened myself up to him and he was the first person to know the real me.I changed a lot of my ways for him. I stopped smoking weed and I started doing my hair and dressing the way he wanted me to. Brian wanted the best for me and I loved him for that.

Before I could leave the fourth message, I hear the door unlock and Brian walked in. He walked into the kitchen and he was pissed off about something, it was all over his face.

"Hey baby." I said as I got up and walked over to him trying to give him a hug. He brushed passed me and walked inside the kitchen towards the sink.

"Joy, why were you calling me like that?" He snapped.

"You said you would be home by eight. I was just worried, that's all."

"I get that. But if I say I'm going to be late, I'll call you. I had a meeting with my upper management, someone tried to file a complaint on me with HR. While I was meeting with them, my phone kept vibrating off the hook. You made me look unprofessional in front of my bosses, you need to chill out with all that calling."

"You should have put the phone on silent." I thought to myself.

"What's this?" he asked sounding a little irritated pointing towards the kitchen table.

"I cooked your favorite meal, it's our six-month anniversary."

"I already ate. Just wrap my plate up, I'll eat it tomorrow. Clean up this stuff and meet me upstairs, I'm tired."

 He brushed passed me, left out the kitchen and made his way upstairs.

I was slightly pissed off. Brian didn't say thank you or anything. He didn't even notice what I was wearing and it took a lot for me to even put this on.
 I wrapped his plate up and cleaned up the kitchen, by the time I was done it was close to midnight. I finally made my way into the bedroom and Brian was sound asleep. I was still upset, so I slid in the bed and closed my eyes to go to sleep.

I couldn't get comfortable because I began to feel Brian's hands all on my booty.

"I know, he aint tryna, have sex after he dismissed me downstairs." I thought to myself.

"Turn over!" he commanded.

I was a little reluctant at first, but then I turned over on my back. He climbed on top of me and he inserted his penis inside of me. Initially, I wasn't feeling it at all. I was waiting for him to be done, but I wouldn't dare push him off, he had a long day. I was always told you never deny your man sex, you give it to him no matter how mad you are. I didn't want him out in the streets looking for it from other women. After about ten minutes, he was done. He kissed me goodnight and rolled over at went to sleep; I followed behind him.

The light from outside was shining bright upon my face and I jumped up quickly realizing I had overslept. I look over to Brian's side and he was already gone to work.

"Oh my God?" I panicked. Brian never leaves the house without breakfast and his coffee.

I reached over on the nightstand to grab my phone and I noticed a folded-up piece of paper resting on top.

I opened and it read:

Joy,
Sorry about last night.
Let me take you out tonight.
Happy Anniversary
Love you,
Brian

I started smiling. Brian has his ways about him, but I know he cared about me. I called Brian and left a voicemail message letting him know I'll be ready when he came home. I decided to lay back down for a few more hours, then I would get up and get dressed. I set my alarm for 5:45pm and I fell back a sleep.

My alarm finally went off and I forced myself to get out of bed. I felt a little sluggish, but I was determined to have this date with my man. Brian liked me to look sexy but classy, he liked all my goodies covered and he didn't want my clothes to be too tight. I decided to put on a short sleeve all black maxi dress with my pair of *Steve Madden* black heels. I unwrapped my hair and my hair fell to my shoulders. Brian liked me to wear my hair straight and he liked me to wear it down. I had no problem looking the way he wanted me to look; I was willing to do anything to keep his eyes only on me.

I peeked over at the clock and it was already a quarter till seven, so I decided to watch a little bit of TV and wait for Brian. Brian arrived home about ten minutes after seven.

He walked through the door looking tired, he saw me sitting on the couch watching TV.

"Joy, what's up? Ima go hit the shower and I should be ready in about fifteen minutes." he said as he walked towards the stairs.

"Ok, I said." as I turned back to watch old re-runs of *Living Single.*

We finally made our way out of the house at about eight; Brian cleaned up nice. He put on a short sleeve black button down, with a pair of dark blue jeans and some all black air forces. He was fine. Brian decided to make it up to me by taking me to TGI Fridays and while I was happy to be out, I was tired of going to these little chain restaurants. I missed the types of restaurants Rayshawn use to take me to. None the less, I tried to make the best of it. We ate dinner and had a decent conversation.

"Joy, Ima go to the restroom. I'll leave my card, so you can pay the waitress."

"Alright babe."

He looked so good walking away; I loved that man. My thoughts were interrupted by someone calling my name. I turned around to see who it was and my stomach dropped. Why did he find his way to my table?

"Hey, how you are doing girl?" Jamier asked.

My heart was beating fast. I tried to speak, but my lips wouldn't move. Oh, my goodness he was fine and his body looked nice. He still looked the same, except he had grown a beard. I was nervous and I rubbed my hair down, hoping it still looked decent.

"So how you are doing?" he asked again.

I finally replied. "I'm doing good, how are you?"

"I'm good. So, you're just going to sit there, don't act like no stranger."

I cut my eyes across the room towards the bathroom. "I know. I ain't no stranger, it's just that, um." I looked towards the bathroom again and he followed my eyes.

"Oh, you here with somebody?" he asked.

"Yea, I'm here with my man."

"Oh, that's what's up. Yo get my number from Des, and hit me up sometimes."

"Alright, I will." I said as he walked away.
As soon as Jamier left the table, Brian made his way back to the table and he seemed a little irritated.

"Yo, who was that nigga?" He asked.

"Who are you talking about?"

"That nigga that was just at the table talking to you?"

I was nervous and I couldn't tell Brian the full truth, so I told him a half lie. "Oh, him? We used to go to school together."

"So, what was he doing over here?"

"He was just saying, Hi. That's all."

"Yea, OK. Ain't no nigga just saying, hi."

"Yes, that's all he said was, hi. Why are you acting like that?"

"I ain't got time for you to be trying to play me." He said with his voice raised a bit.

"How am I trying to play you? He used to go to school with me. He said hi, I spoke back and that was it. What did you want me to do?" I snapped back.

"Did you tell him you had a man?"

"Yes, I did."

"I thought you said, he just said hi. So ya'll talked about some other stuff?"

"Brian, he came over and he said, Hi, how are you doing? What you been up to since school? I told him I was doing good and that I was out celebrating my anniversary.

He congratulated me and he went about his way. Why are you tripping? I knew people before you."

"Yea, but you're my girl now. You don't need any male friends." He grabbed his drink and walked out to the car, I followed behind him.

We argued the whole car ride home, he kept trying to twist up my words and then he claimed I was sleeping around with Jamier. A part of me wish Jamier would have never came over to speak. The crazy thing is I didn't even do anything to warrant him acting this way, but this was Brian. He didn't like other guys looking at me, he didn't like other guys talking to me or me talking to them. He claimed that's how his ex-cheated on him because she was too friendly with men.

As soon as we got in the house he demanded to see my phone. I gave it to him just to shut him up because I knew he wouldn't find anything. He found him a seat on the couch and proceeded to go through my phone.

"Why are you doing this?" I asked as I stood at the end of the couch.

"Why was he at the table?"

"I already told you, he was just saying hi. You are tripping tonight."

"Man, you know how ya'll women do. Ya'll see a new dude and ya'll be ready to cheat."

"Whatever, Brian. I ain't your exes. Ain't nobody trying to cheat on you." I walked passed him and went up the stairs towards our bedroom.

I couldn't believe he was acting like that. Brian has his ways about him and those women did a number on him because he was so insecure. I think he had me beat and I didn't really trust men at all. I made my way to the closet, where I pulled off my clothes, grabbed my robe and walked back into the bedroom. When Brian came into the bedroom, he tossed my phone across the bed.

"Don't ever disrespect me like that. I love you and I'm not trying to get played." he came over and put his hands around my waist.

Usually I'll say something back, but this time I was silent.

"Joy, you know I've been hurt bad. I don't need that mess with you." He confessed.

"I already told you Brian, you don't have to worry about that, I love you too."

He kissed me on my lips and he started feeling on my butt. He pushed me down on the bed and then he started kissing me from my head down to my toes. We made love that night. Brian wasn't perfect, he did have his ways about him, but he loved me and I wanted to keep loving him.

I never had a man love me like he did and Brian wanted me all to himself; that's something I always wanted. After what happen tonight, I made a promise never to have Brian question my loyalty.

Chapter 14

"A little Fun ain't never hurt nobody! Yeah right!"

Over the next couple of months, Brian watched me like a hawk. If I needed to go anywhere he wanted to go with me, and to minimize the arguments I just didn't bother with it. There wasn't anything out in the streets for me anyway. I wanted Brian to know I was different and that I would never screw him over.

I was in the kitchen preparing dinner when I heard my cellphone ringing from the other room. I raced into the other room to grab my phone. Brian hated when I didn't answer his phone calls, but to my surprise it was Shantel. Life had changed for the both of us; She had another baby with Des. Desmond Jr. was born back in April; I missed my sister. When I first got with Brian, Shantel and I use to hang out quite often, while he was at work. But, because of his insecurities these past few months, I haven't been able to see her or the kids. All the drama that we both had going on, we barely talked on the phone. I was glad to see her name flash across the screen of my phone.

"Hello!" I said into the phone.

"Joy, get me out of this house, before I go crazy!" she screamed into the phone.

"What's going on, girl?"

"What ain't going on? I need a break! I'm here with these kids all day every day, by myself. I need some adult fun and Des going out with the boys tonight."

"What you tryna do?"

"You know it's a new club downtown. I wanna go dance. I heard it be poppin."

"Um, I gotta see. Who's gonna keep the kids?"

"I already asked my mom, she said she would."

"What! Ms. Ann keeping some kids?" I laughed.

"I know right. She's something else, but she is off tonight and she wanted to see Aaliyah and D.J. So, are we going or what?"

"Let me check with Brian, because you know how he do. He doesn't like me out especially at the club."

"Ok, let me know. Call me back Joy!"

"Alright, I'll call you in a bit."

Brian came home from work and he seemed to be in a better mood than he has been in lately. I was hoping that it worked in my favor for tonight. I went ahead and fixed his plate and we sat down together to have dinner.

"You seem to be in a better mood today. How was work?" I asked.

"It was cool. My team finally reached our goal after we've been struggling for so long, so I may receive a bonus."

"Oh, that's good babe. I'm happy for you. Do you have any plans for us tonight?"

"Naw, why?"

I was so nervous about asking him, but I did anyway.

"Shantel called me and she wants us to go out, to like a club. I wanted to run it by you to see if it was cool."

"I don't know. All them niggas be out there, I don't know."

"Please? Please? I haven't seen Shantel in a while, and I promise I'll be back at a decent time. If you let me go this time, I won't ask again."

I could tell he didn't really want me to go, but I kept begging and pleading. To my surprise he finally said it was cool; He gave me a list of rules though. I had to be back home by one. I had to call him when I got to Shantel house and he wanted to speak to her. I had to call him when I arrived at the club, and I agreed to everything just so I could go.

I was so excited. I haven't been to a club since I use to dance and I was so happy to get out of the house. I put on some dark blue jeans and a plain white V-neck t-shirt. I pulled my hair back with a white headband and I put on a pair of black flats. I had to make sure my outfit was "Brian Approved" and I knew a dress was out of the question. I was going to borrow one of Shantel's dresses.

I kissed Brian on my way out the door and he yelled "Be back at one!" as I closed the door. I was free, I was finally free. I got into my car, turned up the radio and *Ludacris' "Money Maker"* was blasting through my speakers; I was about to have a night of fun. I pulled up to Shantel's house and she was half-naked. You couldn't even tell she just gave birth to a son. She dropped weight just as quickly as she put it on.

Shantel had on a hot pink belly shirt, some dark blue jean booty shorts and she paired it with some pink high heel sandals. Although I was much bigger than Shantel, she did have a yellow short sleeved dress that I could squeeze in. The dress was tight, came about three inches above my knee and the front draped so my cleavage was exposed. This was a dress I knew Brian wouldn't approve of, but tonight I wanted to be free.

We pulled up to the club and it was packed, the line was wrapped around the building. I could hear *Yung Joc's "It's Going Down"* from inside the club, the DJ was already jamming; so, tonight was about to be a blast.

Before we made our way out of the car, Shantel offered me two shots of grey goose and she gave me her blunt,I decided to take a couple of puffs. I grabbed my phone and called Brian, letting him know I was good. We realized the line was just too long, and we didn't feel like waiting so we skipped the line and paid for VIP.

We finally made our way inside the club and it was packed; People were standing shoulder to shoulder. We made our way to our booth and ordered a bottle; we took a few more shots. Then I noticed Desmond over in the next booth with a couple of guys and some girls.

"Shan, did you know Des was going to be out here?" I asked.

" No! He said he was going out with the boys, but he didn't say they we're going clubbing. Where you see him at?"

I pointed to the booth next to us. "He's over there."

"I'm about to go over there, come with me."

We walked over to Desmond's booth, him and his boys were crunk, then I noticed Jamier. *"Why did he have to be so fine?"* I said to myself.

The security guard was acting like he didn't want to let us in the booth, so Shantel had to get one of Desmond's boys to say we were cool. Once that was confirmed, the security guard let us into the booth. Desmond finally noticed us; he gave us hugs and him and Shantel started talking. Desmond offered us some more shots, we threw them back. I couldn't believe Jamier and I were acting like strangers.

The DJ puts on *D.J UNK's "Walk It Out"* and it was over for me and Shantel, we were killing it. In the middle of me "Walking it Out" Jamier finds his way over to me.

"How you been doing?" He yells in my ear over the music.

"I'm good, how are you?" I yell back.

"I miss you." he says as he leans in and kisses me on my neck.

Oh, man it felt so good, but I couldn't let him do it again. "You can't do that Jamier, you know I got a man."

"I know, but I miss you." he pulled me into his arms, sat down on the couch and pulled me on to his lap.

"Jamier, stop!" I said as I tried to get off his lap.

"Joy, just give me one dance" he said as he started grinding on my butt.

The next thing I know, *"Cash Money taking over for the 99 and the 2000."* came blasting through the speakers; It was over for me. I gave Jamier the lap dance of his life, it took me back to my stripping days. The D.J played hit after hit and Jamier and I was pretty much stuck together the entire night.
We kissed a couple of times and he tried a couple of times to put his hands up my dress; I almost let him, it just felt so good. He had me going, but then I remembered Brian and I had to stop him.

"Last Call for Alcohol! You got twenty minutes to grab you a drink." the hype man said over the microphone.

I got up from Jamier's lap, pulled my phone out of my purse and noticed it was almost 2:00am, I had 103 missed calls from Brian. I was having so much fun, I lost track of time. My mood went from happy to nervous and sad. *"Dang, I messed up."* I didn't even say anything to Jamier, I just walked over to Shantel and told her I had to go. She said she would just leave with Desmond; I gave her a hug and found my way out of the club. I was tore up, but I made it to my car. I hopped in the car and rushed home, hoping Brian would be asleep. When I pulled into my parking space, I noticed the living room light was on.

"Dang, he still up? I'm not ready to hear his mouth." I sat in the car trying to sober up and get myself together. I was trying to figure out my story, what was I going to tell him? I finally got myself together and I was nervous. I pulled myself out of the car and walked up to the door. I tried to slide my key into the lock, but Brian opened the door for me.

"So, you're going to disrespect me like that?" He scolded.

"Disrespect you like, what?" I said as I walked into the house and he closed the door behind me.

"Why you didn't answer your phone?"

"I lost track of time. We were dancing, having a good time and I forgot all about my phone."

"Oh, so you were letting them niggas dance up on you?" He said as he pushed me up on the door.

"No, Shan and I was dancing." I said trying to move passed him, but he wouldn't let me.

"And, why you're dressed like a hoe? You didn't leave the house like that."

"Dang, I forgot to change my clothes back." I thought to myself.

"When I got over to Shan's house she said she had a dress for me to wear, I tried it on and I liked it. So, I wore it."

"But you know I don't like you wearing mess like that, out here looking like a slut! And you came back drunk, you out here looking trashy!"

"Brian, whatever." I said. I tried to push pass him again, but he grabbed my arm and pushed me back up against the door. He then grabbed my cheeks and squeezed them together, using a lot of his strength.

"I am not playing with you. My girl ain't going to be out here doing no hoe stuff." he yelled.

I tried to scream, but he was squeezing then so tight, nothing came out. So, I slapped him in the back of the head; that caused him to squeeze tighter and then he bit me on my lip. Tears started flowing down my eyes.

"Don't you ever put your hands on me Joy, don't get knocked out!" then he took his other hand and put his hand between my legs. I knew Brian was about to be furious.

"You said you wasn't dancing with any niggas, so why are you wet? You're a hoe, still doing hoe stuff. What nigga was you laying up with? Was it that nigga from the restaurant?"

He never let me respond to his questions. He just kept going off about the guy from the restaurant, because that's the only guy he remembers me speaking to. I was panicking because he didn't let my cheeks go, I had never seen this side of Brian. I know he has a temper, but I would've never thought he would ever get physical with me.

"I tried to be cool. Tried to let you have some fun with your friends, but no you can't even do that without disrespecting me. You don't know how to listen. Go take your drunk behind upstairs, take that little hoe dress off and go take a shower. Meet me in the bedroom; since you want to look like a hoe, let's do some hoe stuff."

He finally let my cheeks go and I fell to the floor; all I could do was cry. The tears continued to fall as I slowly picked myself up from the floor and made my way upstairs.

"Why didn't you answer the phone? Why were you drinking so much? Why didn't you keep track of the time?"

I replayed the night over and over in my head wishing I had made better choices.

I walked into the bathroom and glanced at myself in the mirror. My hair was all over my head, my eyes were red and puffy and my cheeks were sore. I rubbed my hands across my lip and I could taste a little blood on the inside of my lip; I started crying again.

"Joy, why couldn't you just do right? Brian loves you, why can't you just do right by him. Why do you want to mess something up with him?" I couldn't help but blame myself for what happened tonight.

I acted careless, irresponsible and foolish. Brian wouldn't have done anything like this if I would have done what he asked of me. I needed to let him know I was sorry and that I would never ever do anything like this again. I wanted to have a little fun, but look what fun got me.

I turned off the shower, grabbed my towel, dried off and slipped on my over-sized t-shirt; brushed my hair into a ponytail. I looked at myself in the mirror again, I looked a mess. I walked out of the bathroom into the bedroom, Brian was sitting on the bed and then he started talking calmly.

"Joy, I'm sorry. I let my anger get the best of me. I'm so used to being done wrong that when things don't add up I get suspect. I love you, if you just work with me, do what I ask you to do and don't ever disrespect me, I'll never hurt you again."

I walked over to him and bent down on my knees in front of him. "No, babe it's all my fault, I acted stupid tonight. I promise I will never disrespect you. Whatever you need from me, I'll do. I love you with all my heart and I'm never going anywhere."

I reached up, pulled his shorts down and to seal my promise I began to give him oral sex. I loved pleasing him and I knew this would show him just how sorry I was. Brian loved me and I just needed to stop doing stupid things. He was a good man, he was faithful and he provided for me; all I needed to do was respect him and do what he says. I know I wanted to have a little fun tonight, but that little fun brought me pain; it wasn't worth it. Brian has my best interest at heart, you just don't hurt a man who loves you.

Chapter 15

"My Failures"

It's been about two weeks since the night I went out with Shantel. I've done everything in my power to keep Brian happy and surprisingly we barely argued. I was on my way downstairs to fix his breakfast, but I found myself in the bathroom hugging the toilet again. Over the past couple of weeks, when I woke up to fix Brian's breakfast I found myself in the bathroom throwing up. It first happened the night after going out with Shantel, I figured I was just hung over but it's been happening for the past two weeks and I'm starting to believe I'm pregnant. My breast has been sore and now that I think about it, I haven't had my period this past month. If I was pregnant, I know it would make Brian so happy, he's always wanted a child of his own. I got myself together and I go downstairs to fix Brian's breakfast and I find him sitting on the couch watching TV.

I went and found a seat next to him.

"Hey, can I ask you a question?"

"Yea!" he said keeping his eyes glued to the TV.

"Do you want to have a family with me?" I asked.

He took his eyes off the TV and looked at me. "Yea, why?"

"Over the past week or so I've been throwing up every morning, I think I might be pregnant."

His face lit up "Yo, are you for real?"

"Yes, I think so. I've been nauseous for a while. I'm going to call around to find a doctor"

"That's what's up. Yo, I can't believe that Ima be a dad." He said.

He kissed me. His face lit up and I was so happy that I would be the one to give him his first child. I went into the kitchen and made our breakfast. I remembered the name off Shantel's doctor, searched for him in the phone book, gave them a call and set up an appointment on my birthday; I was so excited.

Our excitement didn't last long. A couple of days before my birthday and our first doctor's appointment, I miscarried our first child. This was by far one of the worst birthday's I have ever experienced. It was a different type of pain especially when you hope for something and then it's all stripped away from you. As I lay in this hospital bed, I could see the sadness in his eyes. We didn't say anything to each other. He sat in the chair in the corner and looked out of the window. The tears rolled down my cheeks; I felt like a failure.

After the miscarriage Brian grew a little distant, he stayed out later and we barely talked. He started drinking again buying beers and bringing them into the house. Brian was cold and I could see him pulling away from me day by day. I continued cooking and cleaning, but we lived like strangers. We were both dealing with this pain separately and I wish we would have come together. I felt the worse about the miscarriage, I felt like maybe my drinking that night with Shantel caused me to lose the baby. I constantly blamed myself repeatedly. I failed to give Brian the one thing he desired.

▪▪

We were a week away from Christmas. This was going to be our first Christmas together in the townhouse, I was ready to cook, and to exchange gifts. I was even more excited to let Brian know that I was pregnant again.

After the last miscarriage, it took a toll on our relationship, but we were slowly coming back together. We talked about trying again, both of us were nervous but we both needed a family of our own. After Thanksgiving, I started having morning sickness again and I was getting tired from doing little things around the house. I took a home pregnancy test and it was positive. I didn't tell Brian right away, I didn't want to get his hopes up and I miscarry this child, so I kept my mouth shut.

I tried to be careful not to show any symptoms around him and I went to the first Doctor's Appointment alone, which I had to sneak and do.

The Doctor said I was about eight weeks along. I wanted to wait until I was out of my first trimester, but I've made it to week eight and I figured it would be a nice Christmas gift for him.

Brian allowed me to go out to do a little Christmas shopping for Shantel, her kids, him and Ms. Ann. After all that shopping, I decided to pick up some fried fish for dinner because I wasn't up for cooking tonight. I went into the fish market and ordered our food. The place was busy, I guess no one was cooking tonight. They gave me a number, I took a seat and waited for them to call me. I began to feel cramping in my lower stomach. They finally called my number, I grabbed my food and rushed to my car; the cramps became unbearable. I unlocked the door, slid into the driver seat and let the seat back; the pain didn't end.

I began to feel a wetness between my legs. I reached down to touch my thigh and blood stuck to my fingers. I was miscarrying again. Tears swelled up in my eyes.

"Not again, Joy, not again. Why is this happening to me?"

I sat there in disbelief, and the cramps in my stomach kept coming. I didn't have anyone to call, but Brian and what's sad is he doesn't even know I'm pregnant. Now I had to break the news to him like this; I wept until my head hurt.

Brian finally arrived, he pulled me out of my car and put me in his car where I had to sit on a bunch of towels. He looked at me with disgust. After putting me in the car, he grabbed my purse, the food out the car, hopped in the driver's seat of his car and drove me to the hospital.

"So, you were pregnant again?" He asked.

I shook my head yes.

"Why didn't you tell me?"

"I was going to tell you on Christmas. I was going to surprise you, but I didn't tell you right away because I didn't want to get your hopes high."

"You were carrying my child and you didn't let me know or you didn't tell me because it was somebody else's?"

Brian's question threw me off. I was sitting here miscarrying our child and he had the nerve to accuse me of cheating.

"I didn't tell you because I didn't want you hurt if I lost the baby."

"Well, look what's happening now. You just can't stay pregnant? What's wrong with you? Why can't you stay pregnant?"

"I don't know Brian." I said crying hysterically.

"What are you good for if you can't give me a child? Maybe it's all those abortions you had or maybe it's because of all those niggas you had sex with raw. But what should I expect from a hoe."

His words stung. I couldn't believe he was being so insensitive; I was hurt too. I wanted more than anything to give him a child, but he was hitting below the belt. I shared those things with him in confidence and now he was throwing my past back in my face.

"I told you to lose some weight after the last miscarriage, you don't ever listen. Now I'm losing another child. Dang Joy, what's wrong with you? Why can't you give me a child?!" He yelled.

I could see the pain in his eyes and little did he know this hurt me just as much as it hurt him. After everything Brian said, he had me wondering if my past played a part in my ability to carry a child. Maybe he was right and maybe it was all my fault. A woman was supposed to give her man a child and I couldn't; I was such a failure. Once we arrived at the hospital, he helped me get signed in and once I was admitted, he left me to face this miscarriage alone. I didn't see Brian until I was discharged from the hospital.

Chapter 16

"Walking on Egg Shells"

I turned over in the bed after taking an evening nap and Brian's side of the bed was still empty; I was relieved. My head was throbbing and after this morning, I was glad to be alone. I walked in the bathroom and I noticed my reflection in the mirror. There I stood a 19-year-old, girl and the man I loved blacked my eye.

Five months after the miscarriage, my relationship with Brian took a turn for the worst. Brian lost his job two weeks after the miscarriage, for taking too many unauthorized days off. The loss of our child and the loss of his job sent Brain down a deep spiral of anger and depression. He was getting unemployment, but he felt like that wasn't good enough. His drinking became his comfort again and he was drinking so much he smelled like an entire bottle of alcohol. He was always angry especially at me, and there was nothing I could do right. I felt like a stranger in my own home. I walked around on egg shells, afraid that if I breathed too heavy he would snap.

Brian was verbally abusive too, and his words cut deep as if he had picked up a knife himself and stabbed me in the back.

If you let him tell it, I was a whore, slut, fat, ugly, black monkey, bitch, stupid, dumb and the list goes on; it got worse when he was drunk. When he was really tore up he got physical with me.
He would push me, shove me, and punch me; no place on my body was off limits.

I didn't have any contact with anyone outside of Brian. He cut off my cellphone, and the house phone, he would unplug and take with him whenever he left the house. They repossessed his car and because my car was paid off, he drove it like he owned it.

Brian wanted to be in complete control of me in every possible way. He controlled how we had sex, it was done when he wanted and how he wanted regardless of how I felt. The drunk sex was the worst, to have a man lying on top of you smelling like a can of beer, his sweat smelled like alcohol, and his sex was sloppy. I cringed every time he would touch me and every time we had sex.

Brian broke me down and I cried daily. As much pain as he put me through; I couldn't be without him. He was right in a sense, I was fat. I had no family, I had so many abortions that I couldn't stay pregnant.

I've slept with so many men and I'm an ex-stripper. When I think about all that, it's makes staying with Brian the best thing for me.

He knew about my past and he accepted me. I felt like he needed me and I needed him. We both had some issues and I figured I could help him deal with his.

He had loss so much these past few months and I knew if I would have left he would get even more depressed. I didn't want that for him so, I took the wrath of his anger in my efforts to change him.

I looked at my eye, my busted lip and just wanted Brian to get better. He was hurting me over some of the smallest things and we got into the fight this morning because of nothing. He came home pissed off and took whatever happened outside out on me. I had now become numb to the pain. I got myself together and went down stairs to try to fix me something to eat. I was glad to be home alone, I didn't know where Brian was, but at this moment I didn't care. I fixed me a sandwich and made my way back upstairs to eat and I watch a little TV.

My mood was interrupted when I overheard Brian come into the house. He was loud and talking on his phone, to someone and when he came into the room, I pretended to be sleep. He continued with the conversation.

"Did I like what?" I heard Brian say into the phone.

"Yea, I enjoyed it all." He chuckled.

"Well, there's more where that came from." he said

"I'll be back over there tomorrow, that's what's up" he laughed.

"I'll hit you up tomorrow." He said as the conversation ended.

My blood was boiling, I wondered who Brian was on the phone with, and what did he enjoy.
I wanted to say something to him, but after what happened this morning, I didn't want to have another fight. So, I left it alone and made a mental note.

I felt him slide into the bed and I cringed. I heard him calling for me, but I ignored him. I was laying on my stomach, he climbed on top of me and he slid his penis inside of me; I felt disgusted. Each time he would breath in my ear, I smell the foul odor on his breath. His breath smelt like beer and vagina. He tried to kiss me in my mouth, but his kisses were sloppy and I couldn't stomach his breath. I couldn't believe I was here with this man, he was finally done after what seemed like forever. He climbed off me and he turned over and at went to sleep. I wept for the rest of the night.

· ·

Two days go by, Brian hasn't been home and while I was glad at first, I became a little worried. He had never done anything like this and there was no way for me to contact him.I felt like a prisoner. I had no one to talk to, but the walls. To pass the time I decided to watch TV, and I found some old re-runs of *Martin,* hoping Brian would come home soon.

"Get up. What you doing sleep?" I hear Brian's voice as he punches me in the arm to get up. I realized I had dozed off in the middle of *Martin.*

I finally came to and I sat up on the couch.

"What time is it?" I asked Brian.

"Time for you to make me some dinner." he snapped.

I could smell the beer on his breath.

"Where have you been these past couple of days?" I asked him.

"Don't worry about it. Go ahead and get up. I'm hungry."

"So, you're not going to tell me where you've been? I was worried."

"See, there you go. I try to be nice and you always take it there. Dang, can I just come home to some peace instead of hearing your mouth? I swear you get on my nerves Joy. Talk too much. Shut the hell up sometimes."

I pulled myself off the couch and into the kitchen.

"My bad." I said finding myself walking on those egg shells again. My eyes were watering up and my voice got a little shaky. "What do you want for dinner?"

"Some fried pork chops, rice and gravy and bring me a beer."

"Ok." I walked over to take Brian his beer as he took up my spot on the couch. I went back in the kitchen to cook dinner. I pulled the pork chops out of the freezer and threw them in the microwave to defrost. I glanced over at the clock, it was 9:23pm.

"He should have eaten wherever he was." I thought to myself.

An hour and half later, I served Brian his dinner on the couch. I tried to sit next to him on the couch and he demanded that I give him some space.

"Why are you treating me like this Brian?" I asked

"Cause you ain't nothing but a fat cow. You so fat. Pillsbury Dough girl with all those rolls. Aint nothing sexy about you. If I would've known you would get this fat, I would have left you at the club, get out of my face and go clean the kitchen."

I got up and with tear filled eyes and didn't bothered saying anything to him. I made my way back into the kitchen to clean up the dishes. I hated feeling this way and I hated living in fear, I was afraid that Brian would snap anytime. I was tired of walking on Egg shells, I needed Brian to return back to the man I first fell in Love with.

Chapter 17

"Text Messages and Pain"

I peeked back in the living room and Brian was asleep on the couch. I walked back into the living room and figured this would be the perfect time to look through his phone. I wanted to see what I could find, because I had a feeling he was cheating on me.

I walked up to the couch to see if I could see the phone and I noticed it was on the floor next to the couch. I was nervous, and there were butterflies in my stomach; My hands were shaking. I grabbed the phone and ran into the downstairs bathroom.
I locked the door behind me.
Brian had one of those iPhone, so it made looking through his messages easy for me. I got into the phone and scrolled over to messages and there was only one name in the messages "Stacy". My stomach dropped and my heart started beating faster. I was not ready for this, but I needed to know if he was cheating on me or not.

I clicked on her name and when I opened the messages the first message that caught my eye read

9:15p **Stacy**: I love you, Ima miss you too. Brian see you when you get back
9:25 p **Brian**: Luv ya 2

My heart sank into the bottom of my chest and I felt a sting to my heart. I couldn't believe Brian said he loved another girl. I decided to scroll up to read all the messages, but there weren't that many. It seemed like he deleted the messages because the first messages started a few days or so ago.

May 2 ,2007

8:15p **Stacy**: Hey boo!

8:18p **Brian**: What's good

8:22p **Stacy**: What you doing tonight?

8:28p **Brian**: You ☺

8:29p **Stacy**: Oh really? ;-)

8:31p **Brian**: You know you miss this, you miss me

8:33p **Stacy**: Yeah, I miss you so much baby when are you coming by? It's been a while.

8:35p **Brian**: I'm tryna come tonight, if that's cool

8:36p **Stacy**: Yea, you can. You know I moved last weekend. I have to give you my new address.

8:38p **Brian**: Oh, you got us a new place. That's what's up, send it to me.

8:40p   **Stac**y: You could stay with me anytime you like ☺ 7750 Pointer Circle Apt 3B, see you in a few

8:52p   **Brian**: put on something sexy, you know what I like

8:55p   **Stacy**: I will ☺

May 3, 2007

4:43p **Brian**: Hello

4:45p **Stacy**: Hey baby

4:50p   **Brian**: You was dripping wet last night lol. Ima have to take you off the market.

4:52p **Stacy**: I missed you. You sure you're ready to be with me. I enjoyed you too last night, can you come back tonight?

4:54p **Brian**: Yea, I'll be over. Give me a couple of hrs. I'll hit you up when I'm on the way.

4:55p **Stacy**: Ok.

8:16p **Brian**: I'm on the way.

8:18p **Stacy**: Ok babe.

May 4, 2007

8:30a **Stacy**: Good morning, Baby.

9:48a **Brian**: What's up?

9:53a **Stacy**: I was thinking about you. I know you said you had to take care of your mom last night, so you couldn't stay. Do you think you could get away sometime today?

10:03a **Brian:** let me see what I can do, I'll hit you up

10:04a **Stacy**: see you soon babe

11:35a **Brian**: My brother came to take over my shift with my mom, so I'm on the way, put on something sexy

11:37a **Stacy**: Anything for you ☺

May 6, 2007

8:50p **Brian:** I love spending time with you, and I enjoyed being with you these past couple of days. Ima be out of town for a few days on business. I'll hit you up when I get back. Ima miss you baby.

9:15p **Stacy**: I love you, Ima miss you too. Brian see you when you get back

9:25 p **Brian**: Luv ya 2

I couldn't stop crying. I could barely breathe, and now I know where Brian was these past few days. The tears came down hot and heavy and I could barely get myself together. I went from sad, to mad to sad, angry to jealous, to angry again, all in the span of one minute. He was a liar, lying about his mother, knowing she was dead. I had to take a few deep breaths until I got myself together. I stood up off the toilet trying to figure out my next move. Brian was in a whole relationship with this Stacy girl, as if I wasn't even in the picture. Something in me told me to call her and cuss her out. My anger got the best of me and I saw the word "Call" next to her name, I clicked the word and it dialed her number.

"Hey, baby did you make it to the hotel yet?" she said cheerfully into the phone.

"I'm not your baby, I am Brian's girlfriend!" I snapped into the phone.

She chuckled "Oh, really? Oh wow! Wow! Brian said he didn't have a girlfriend."

"Now that you know, I need you to leave my man alone. Don't call him no more, we good over here."

"Brian ain't said nothing to me about having a girlfriend and until he tells me to stop calling, I will!" She snapped back and before I could get another word out, she hung up the phone.

I tried to call her back, but she turned her phone off and that pissed me off even more. I opened the bathroom door and Brian was still sound asleep on the couch. My anger got the best of me and I completely lost it. After all the tipping toeing I've been doing around the house, making sure not to piss him off and he cheats on me. All I saw was red. I threw the phone at him and climbed on top of him and starting punch him like a stranger who stole my purse. He finally came to.

"You bastard!" I screamed. "I'm locked up in this house being faithful to you and you out sleeping around on me."

"Yo, what the hell?" he yelled pushing me off him and I hit the floor.

I stood up and got right back in his face. "I hate you, I hate you, I hate you!" I screamed.

"Get out of my face, you stupid hoe! I don't even know what you're talking about." He pushed me out of his face, and started walking towards the bathroom.

I followed him towards the bathroom "I saw it on your phone."

"Why are you going through my phone? he shoved me out of his way. "Stop following me, don't piss me of Joy."

He turned around to walk into the bathroom and I smacked him in the back of the head. He turned around quickly and punched me right in the mouth. He hit me so hard, I fell to the ground and he kicked me in the stomach.

"You, fat stupid hoe, stay out of my stuff. You so stupid, you'll think twice before you put your hands on me again."

He kicked me in the stomach again. He then went over to the couch and grabbed my car keys and he picked up his phone off the floor and he left out of the door.

I laid there lifeless, my heart and my body ached. Blood dripped from my lip onto the carpet. My head started pounding. I finally found the strength to pull myself off the floor, my legs were hurting and my stomach was in so much pain. I walked slowly back into the bathroom, fearing what would be looking back at me. It seems like I was always in the mirror trying to make sense of the damage Brian caused to my face. My eye was trying to get better and now I had to deal with my jaw. It felt like it could be broken and my lip was even worse than it was a few days ago.

I couldn't even cry; I wanted to but the tears wouldn't come out. I was just so tired of the pain.

"I'm so tired!" I screamed out in the bathroom.

"I'm so tired!" I screamed several times in the bathroom.

Brian was the one sending the text messages and I was the one sitting here in pain. The damage Brian caused was beyond repair. I was in so much pain and I couldn't bear it. It was late outside, but I needed to get to the hospital. My jaw and stomach was hurting badly. I slipped on some sweat pants and got up the courage to ask my neighbor could I use their phone. I went over and knocked on their door and to my surprise they were very helpful for it to be so late. They offered to call the cops, but I told them I didn't want to, I just needed to go to the hospital. My neighbor insisted on driving me to the hospital instead of me waiting for the ambulance.

When we arrived at the hospital, I told my neighbor I would have my sister drive me home. I thanked her and walked into the hospital. I felt so alone. I noticed a phone on the wall and I decided to call Shantel.

To my surprise she answered. "Hello." she said into the phone.

"Shantel, I need you." I said sobbing into the phone.

"Who is this?" she replied.

"It's me, Joy."

"Oh, my goodness, Joy. Where have you been? Are you OK?"

"Shan, Shan, I need you. I'm over at Maple Medical Center, can you please come up here to the hospital? I need you."

"Joy, tell me is everything ok?"

"Please just come, please Shan, I'm so tired, I'm so tired."

"Ok, let me throw some clothes on and I'll be there."

Shantel finally arrived and she couldn't believe her eyes when she seen my face. We just hugged for a least 10 minutes and all I could do was cry. I needed her at that moment.

"What happened, Joy? Where's Brian?" She asked.

"Girl, Brian ain't no good. He's cheating on me and I caught him so we got into a fight, his face worse than mine." I lied, I wasn't ready to confess the abuse to Shantel.

"I'm so tired sis, I don't know what to do. He keeps me up in the house, that's why I haven't talked to you in the past few months. His drinking just got out of control and things got bad. I know he can change and I hope he will change. Some days I want to leave, but I know ain't nobody going to love me like he does."

"I'm so sorry sis, I'm sorry you're dealing with this, hopefully he gets it together so ya'll can make it work."

"I know if he gets his job back, he'll be good. When he lost his job, that's when things got bad. I know he can do better, I hope he gets a job soon."

"Joy Alton." The nurse called for me. She took me in the room and checked my vital signs. She asked me what brought me here and I told her I got into a fight with someone that was trying to steal from me. My lie probably didn't even make sense, considering how my face looked but I couldn't tell her the truth. She asked me was I suffering from domestic violence and I lied again to protect Brian. She told me to go back out into the lobby.

Forty-five minutes later, they called me into the back and the nurse put me in triage. She asked me what happened again and I told her the same story I told the lady who checked my vitals.

"We may need an x-ray of your jaw. You told the nurse that you didn't remember the last time you had your period, could you be pregnant?" The Triage nurse asked.

"Nope, I don't think so. I've been stressed lately, that's probably why my period has been acting up."

"Can you give me a urine sample anyway? We just want to make sure. There is a bathroom down the hall and the cups are inside the bathroom. Fill it up and bring it back down here with you."

I gave the nurse the urine sample and I settled in the bed. I couldn't believe Brian sent me to the hospital with all his foolishness.

"Maybe I shouldn't have even looked at those text messages, then I wouldn't be here, in all this pain."

The nurse came back in and informed me that the doctor was coming in to put some stitches in my lip and that they weren't going to be able to perform the x-ray because my urine sample came back positive for pregnancy. She said the doctor would also examine my jaw and that they were going to do an ultrasound to figure out how far along I was.

Two hours later, they finally discharged me from the hospital. I received stitches in my lip and thank goodness, my jaw wasn't broken it was just real sore, so they prescribed me some Tylenol for it. They informed me that I was about four months pregnant and I needed to follow up with my primary doctor. I couldn't believe it, I didn't have any symptoms, but I was excited none the less. I couldn't wait to tell Brian.

Shantel dropped me off at the townhouse and I thanked her for everything. If no one had my back, I knew Shantel did. My car wasn't outside so I knew Brian wasn't home. I walked inside the house and walked inside the bedroom. I was exhausted; I took off my clothes and laid across the bed. I grabbed the ultrasound picture and all I could do was smile.

"I'm pregnant, and I made it past the first trimester, now we're going to be a real family." I thought to myself.

Chapter 18

"Who do you Choose?"

"Just give us a couple more pushes." I hear the doctor say to me.

"Ok, on the count of ten, I want you to push." The nurse said.

I look over to my side and Brian was there holding my legs. I pushed for about another five minutes and my son was finally out. Tears flowed from my eyes as soon as I heard him cry. They threw him on top of me and I have never been so happy in my life. After twenty-eight hours of labor, and after everything I've been through it was worth it to finally lay eyes on my son. He was born on November 13, 2007 and this day changed our lives forever. Brian kissed me on the forehead. We finally had our family; Everything felt so right.

The nurses grabbed Brian Jr. off me and took him to get cleaned up; they wanted to check his vitals. I laid there tired and in awe at the same time. I still couldn't believe I was someone's mother.

I finally gave Brian a son. I laid there thinking back on the past few months and about everything we've been through to get to this place. It was rocky, but we made it.

After finding out I was pregnant, I was beyond excited and I couldn't wait to share the news with Brian. Brian came home the next day and I showed him the ultrasound and let him know he was going to be a dad. Brian had mixed emotions, he wanted to be happy but he feared a miscarriage again. After realizing he could have hurt our child, he apologized for punching me and kicking me. I accepted his apology and I chose to move forward to focus on our child. He said he knows he needs help with his temper and drinking and he asked if I could be by his side while he gets the help he need. He said he's just stressed out and his life over these pasts few months has pulled him into a depression. He promised he would get better and I believed he could; I wanted to help him get better. I wanted our family.

The next couple of weeks things did get better. He found him job at *Auto-Zone,* and his drinking slowed down. He was at home more and we we're getting along for the most part. Our sex life even got better; we were connecting emotionally again. I was so happy and I knew he could get better, I knew if I hung in there Brian would be the man I knew he can be. He would be the father I needed him to be.

When I was five and half months pregnant, he switched up on me again. He started controlling my every move and he started cheating again with Stacy. I was stressed out because all my energy was put into trying to get Brian to act right.

He didn't get physical with me because he didn't want to hurt the baby, but his mouth was still reckless. He stopped taking me to my doctor's appointments, but when I asked Shantel to take me, he got pissed off about that, so he started taking me again. Brian was barely home and Stacy and I was battling over him. She became a thorn in my side.

When I was about eight months pregnant, Brian didn't come home for like three days straight and usually when he didn't come home, I knew he was laid up with Stacy. She didn't mind being his other woman and after all the arguing we did, she didn't plan on letting him go even after she found out he had me pregnant. I thought I was stuck like glue, but she was too. I was tired of her and him but I wasn't about to let her take my man or break up my family. I had enough, and I was going to get my man, pregnant and all.

I called a taxi to drive me over to Stacy's place. I arrived at her apartment complex and there was my *Mercedes* pulled into a parking spot. I got out and I waddled up the stairs to her apartment. I didn't have a plan of action, but I was just tired and I was going to get my man. I was slightly nervous, but there was no turning back. I knocked on the door and used my other hand to cover the peep hole so they couldn't look out. The door open and to my surprise Brian answered the door with only a pair of shorts on.

"Yo, what you are doing here?" he asked angrily.

"I'm so tired, Brian. I'm tired of your mess." I yelled on purpose so Stacy could hear me.

"Joy, go the hell home. I don't even know why you came over her, stop tripping." he yelled back.

"No! No!, No! I'm not going back home! I'm pregnant with your son and you laid up here with this stupid hoe." I screamed.

He closed the door and stepped outside and had the nerve to try to console me. He tried to wrap his arms around me but I pulled away.

"Joy, go home, don't be coming over here with this mess."

"I'll leave if you're coming with me. Go get the keys and let's go home."

"Naw, you go home, however you got here." He snapped back.

"Brian, I hate you." I screamed as I raised my hand to slap him, but he grabbed my hand and twisted my wrist.

"Don't you start, don't put your hands on me!" He yelled twisting my wrist harder and then he let it go.

I started rubbing my wrist where the pain was.

"Why won't you come home?"

Stacy opened the door. "He doesn't want to go home with you, you stupid slut! Don't you get it? He wants to be with me!" Stacy yelled.

Brian pushed her back in.

"You the stupid hoe, sleeping with somebody else's man. You're lucky I'm pregnant or I would lay you out, dumb hoe!" I snapped back.

She tried to reach over Brian to get to me and I lost it and I tried to reach over and slap her; Brian grabbed my hand before it landed on her face. Brian pushed her back inside, they exchanged a few words and he came back to the door.

"Yo, man you gotta leave. I ain't got time for this right now."

"So, you just going to stay with her? I'm pregnant with our son and you just going to stay here with her." Tears rolled down my cheeks.

"Go home Joy!" He said turning away to walk back into the house.

I grabbed him by the arm. "Brian don't do this, look at me, are you really going to choose that hoe over us, over your family?"

He looked at me dead in my face and what he said shook me to the core. "I don't know who I'm going to choose."

I started breathing heavy, my heart was torn. Tears ran down my cheeks. I tried to hug him, but he pushed me away.

"Go home, Joy, just leave."

"Really Brian, you don't know who you're going to choose? Tell me what does she do for you that I'm not doing? Tell me what can I do to make you come home. Please come home with me, I'm giving you a son, we need you, we need you, Brian please, please Brian, don't leave me, don't leave us." I pleaded.

"Just go home, Joy." He said as he walked in the house and closed the door.

I was crying profusely, snot and everything was running down my face. I started knocking on the door and I probably knocked for at least five minutes straight and no one answered, he never came back. Brian made his choice after he left me outside in the cold pregnant with his child. Every time I had hope that Brian would change, he let me down every time. I didn't really know how to feel, on the ride home. I replayed the altercation over and over in my head and I couldn't believe he left me to be with her.

What was it about her that made him want her over me? What did she have that I lacked? Why wasn't I good enough?

Even though I was giving him a child, that still didn't make him want me over her. I cried for the rest of the day.

Two weeks before I had B.J, Brian finally came home. He stayed over with Stacy for about two weeks. When he was with her, we had no communication. I just knew we were done until he showed back up. When he came home, he told me Stacy put him out, they got into a bad argument and she told him to leave. He said that's when he realized he missed me and our family and he needed to come back home. He said he always loved me and he got caught up with Stacy after the miscarriages and losing his job; she was there for him when I wasn't.

He said she was no longer in the picture, he wanted his family back and that I was the one he chose. He promised to be better and I wanted his promise to really come true.

I look at Brian sitting in the chair holding our son and I can see how happy he is; it makes everything we've been through worth it. Brian chose me. Brian chose his son. Brian chose our family and I was happy.

Chapter 19

"Hell, on Earth"

"Happy Birthday to you. Happy birthday to B.J. happy birthday to you." We all sung in unison to B.J

"Blow your candle out baby." I said to B.J.

"Yay!" Everyone shouted.

"Who wants cake?" I asked as I grabbed the knife to slice the cake.

It was B. J's second birthday and I was throwing him a small party at our apartment. B.J was a wonderful child, and he didn't give me any problems. He was so handsome and looked nothing like me. He was definitely Brian's child, but I was so glad he acted nothing like his daddy. After seeing Brian's happiness in the hospital, I knew in my heart he would be a good father because a family was all he ever wanted but that wasn't the case.

When we brought B.J home from the hospital he helped a little, but I carried the load and majority of the time I felt like a single mother. Brian was back to his old ways and things got bad quickly. His drinking was out of control, which caused him to lose his job at *Auto Zone*.

The money I had saved from the club was long gone from the last time Brian lost his job. We were evicted from the townhouse, so we had to move into a public housing complex. I was so tempted to go back and dance, I wasn't used to struggling like this. My old manager at *Taco Bell* let me come back part-time and I applied for welfare. I got on every kind of assistance I could, to help my family. Brian didn't want me working, but this time he didn't have a choice, we were struggling bad and I had to make sure B.J was taken care of. Brian made sure he drove me to work and he picked me up and I couldn't do more than five hours a day. He wanted me to let him have control of the money, which I foolishly did and he blew every cent.

On top of having no money, Brian was constantly cheating on me, and I fought a couple of women behind him. Brian infected me with a couple of STD's which I was able to cure, but I was afraid he was going to give me something I wouldn't be able to cure. I tried to make him use condoms, but he refused to put them on because he didn't like the way they felt. Which led to me getting pregnant again, but like my other pregnancies, I miscarried that child and that added more pain to an already pain filled relationship.

I tried to get my tubes tied, but my doctor said I was too young, Brian took his chances but thankfully I didn't get pregnant again.

Then there were the fights, which led me to drinking beer to cure my own pain. We would cuss each other out like strangers on the street. He used his words to beat me down and I felt low about myself.

We fought about other women, we fought about him not taking care of B.J, we fought because we we're drunk. We did all this in front of B.J. Some of these fights led to me being hospitalized, I had a broken rib cage, and he broke my wrist. We were toxic. As painful as things had become, I still couldn't leave Brian, he made it very clear that no one would love me like he did and I believed him.

"Here, Aaliyah grab this piece of cake and take one to D.J".
"Here's your cake B.J you can go eat it in the room."

"Daddy! Daddy!" B.J said as he runs up to Brian. Brian walked into the kitchen with two bags from *Toys- R- Us*. He picks BJ up.

"Happy birthday, B.J, daddy loves you. I got you some toys, go eat your cake and I'll bring you the toys in a few." He put him down and BJ grabbed his cake from the table and ran out of the kitchen.

"What's up, Joy?" He said to me smelling like beer. His eyes were blood shot red, he was probably drunk.

"You're two hours late and who bought those toys? I know you ain't got no money." I said to him.

"Damn, Joy, don't start. Just know I found a way to get my son his gifts." He tried to lean in and kiss me. I backed away.

"Why you starting that mess again? Come give me a kiss." He pulled me close to him.

"Stop, Brian!" I tried to push him away. He kissed me on my neck and then he pushed me off.

"Dang, I can't even kiss you?" he said as I smelled the liquor on his breath.

"You need to make us a priority." I snapped.

"Are you drunk Brian, at BJ's party?"

"Joy, I'm good, chill out!"

"Whatever." I said rolling my eyes at him.

"Let me go give him these toys, I got to run out, I'll be back."

"You not going to stay? You show up two hours late and you're not going to stay?" I was getting upset, I was tired of him dissing B.J.

"I said, I'll be back. Chill out dang, he good. You ain't never satisfied. You always got a problem with something." He walked out of the kitchen.

"Oh, hey Brian." Shantel says as she walks into the kitchen

"What's up Shan?" Brian says as he turns around and makes his way back in the room.

"Girl! That cake was good. I-"she stopped mid-sentence when she noticed the frustration on my face.

"What happened now?"

"He's drunk. Brian couldn't even put the drinking down for one freaking day and he didn't even show up on time and now he's about to leave again." I was irritated.

"Joy, don't even sweat it, he came. BJ is happy, don't let it get to you, you know how Brian is."

"Yea, but I thought he would at least do better for B. J's birthday."

"Yea, and he did. He's here, isn't he? He could've been laid up somewhere but he made it to his son's party, he did good."

"He's two hours late."

"At least he came, give him some credit, Joy."

"Yea, ok, if you say so."

I noticed Brian leaving out the door and I didn't bother saying anything to him. I was still pissed regardless of what Shantel says.

"You have to stop stressing out about Brian and just let him do him."

"I'm just tired of going through hell with Brian, and I know you tired of dealing with the same crap; the drama, the other women." I asked as I sat down at the kitchen table, she took a seat next to me.

"Girl,yes I'm tired. He's my family and the kid's daddy. We've been together forever, he's all I ever known and he's all I ever been with. We do go through a lot of stuff, but what relationship doesn't. I mean if I leave him, it'll just be the same crap with the next man."

"I love Brian, but I'm tired of him controlling me, I tired of everything, the women, everything. I thought B.J would change him but it's still the same mess. Sometimes I want to leave but then something forces me to stay. I don't know Shan, I just know I'm tired. I want to be happy."

"Men are going to be Men though, they all are the same. If you leave Brian, the next dude might not be any different. Every man comes with crap, but Brian's loves you. He comes back home to you every time, that must count for something."

"You're right, he does come home and I think he can get better. It's just so many things that happened to him and me over the past years, that he has to work through."

"Right, after all those women and all the things ya'll been through, he come back to you because he knows he loves you. They say love is pain, so pain is going to come with the love, so don't trip so much."

"How do you deal with the other woman? I'm tired of them."

"If they get out of line, you just kick their butts, because I don't play about my man. Ain't nobody going to love Desmond, like I love him."

"You're a mess, but you're right ain't nobody taking Brian from me."

"You know me and Des been through some of everything, but he's still here; we've been together for some years now. Love takes time. Sometimes you have to deal with mess and drama, but when it's real nothing will break ya'll apart."

"You're so right. I think about everything I've been through with my mom and my grandparents, Brian still wanted me. He still loved me and I don't know if anyone else will care about me like he has. It has to get better, I want it to get better."

"It will, Brian just has to grow up Joy and once he does, ya'll will be good. So, don't trip and stop stressing so much." She leaned over and hugged me.

"I hear you sis, I just want my family back together, and I love him so much."

Shantel gave me hope and helped me see that love will be pain. I saw it with my mom and I saw it with other people, but she also gave me hope that once Brian grows up that things will be better. I decided to focus on us getting better instead of the drama. I know Brian loved me because if he didn't he wouldn't still be here. He accepted my past, he knew the real me and I don't ever think anyone else will be able to understand me or my past. Shantel and I talked about some other stuff and we laughed and cried with each other.

"You want another piece of cake?" I asked Shantel as I stood up to grab another piece.

"Naw, I'm good, I think we about to go"

I looked over at the clock and it was a quarter to twelve. We exchanged hugs, kisses and I love you's. She gathered her children and they left. I closed the door behind them and went into B. J's room and put him to sleep. He was such a sweet child, he was the best thing that ever happened to me. I laid him down in his toddler bed, I kissed him goodnight.

I walked back in the living room and took a seat on the couch and realized Brian still hasn't returned home. I was mad all over again and any negative thought I had about Brian came rushing to my mind. It was one thing to do me wrong, but I was so tired of him doing BJ wrong.

I decided to call him on his cell. I called three times and on the third call he finally answered.

"Where are you?" I yelled into the phone before he could say hello.

"Yo, I said I'll be back!" he yelled back.

"That was almost three hours ago, you better not be with no chick!" I screamed even louder into the phone not caring if I woke up B.J.

"I'm on my way home, chill the hell out!" he snapped back.

"Whatever!" I yelled into the phone, hanging up on him.

I was pissed off; my heart was beating fast and I wanted to curse him out. Ugh! Just one day, he couldn't even give us one day, where we could spend time together as a family. He had to be out, laid up with somebody. I grabbed me a beer from the refrigerator, pop it open and took it straight to the head. I was tired of Brian. I decided not to wait up for him. I made my way back into the master bedroom and I crawled into the bed and fell asleep.

I was awakened to kisses on my forehead. When I opened my eyes, I realized it was BJ and that was his way of letting me know he wanted something to eat. I turned over and laid there for a second.

My head was thumping. *"I guess that beer did have on me and I can't believe Brian didn't come home last night."*

I finally pulled myself out of bed and I made my way down the hall to the kitchen. When I looked in the living room, Brian was passed out on the couch. I rolled my eyes at the sight of him. I fixed BJ some toast and eggs and sat him down in his booster seat at the table.

"Eat up, baby, I'm going to the bathroom. Mommy will be back ok?" I handed him one of his toys to keep him occupied. He nodded his head "yes". He was a sweet child.

I walk into the bathroom noticing I still had yesterday's clothes on. I stripped down and jumped in the shower for a quick five-minutes. I dry off and put on a t-shirt I left hanging on the door. I go over to the faucet and I turn it on as I prepare to brush my teeth and then Brian came in.

"Brian, I'm in here. I'll be out in a second" I said to him but he enters the bathroom anyway.

He goes over, uses the bathroom and then he walks over to the sink where I 'm standing and grabs a handful of my butt.

"Stop!" I snapped.

"Oh, so I can't touch you now?"

"Yea, when you come home at night." I replied back.

"You mine. I can touch you anywhere I like." He started feeling on my breast.

"Brian chill out!" I yelled as I pushed his hand away.

He grabbed me again and he started feeling on my vagina. He pulled me close to him with his other hand and he started kissing me on the neck. I wanted to keep fighting him to stop, but part of me wanted him there. Part of me wanted his touches, part of me wanted to make love to him. He bent me over the sink; we had sex and it felt so good. It hasn't felt this way in a long time. He pulled out and ejaculated on my back. He was done way to soon and he left me wanting more.

"Let's go in the bedroom." I insisted.

"Naw, I'm good, wipe that mess off your back and go make me some breakfast!" He demanded and walked out of the bathroom.

"I'm tired of your----"I stopped midsentence. I wasn't even going to argue with him, but my feelings were hurt. He was constantly hurting my feelings and treating me like crap. He didn't say nice things to me, he treated me like a side whore.

He bent me over the sink, did his business and he went about his business. It hurts that he doesn't want to spend any time with me.

I got myself together and crept out of the bathroom. I see BJ and Brian wrestling in the living room. I walk passed them fast trying not to make eye contact with Brian.

I fixed breakfast and I served Brian; He ate and then he hopped in the shower. BJ and I took up residence on the couch where we watched "*Dora the Explorer*" on T.V. I noticed Brian walking passed us all dressed up. I fought back and forth with myself because I wanted to ask him where he was going, but the other part of me didn't want the confrontation. I couldn't stop the words they came out without warning.

"So, where are you going this time?" I said getting up off the couch.

"Out." He replied.

"Can't you just stay home one day?" My voice was elevated. "I mean just one night with us." I said changing my tone.

He didn't say a thing, he brushed passed me and grabbed my keys.

I blocked the front door.

"Brian, what do I have to do to keep you home?" My voice was shaky as I began to cry.

"Move the hell out of my way, Joy!" He pushed me with his hand and reached for the door knob and I grabbed his hand.

"Brian, stop. Brian, don't keep doing this to me, to us." I yelled as I started punching him in the chest.

He backhanded me right in the face. The power of his slap almost sent me to the ground; I stumbled but I didn't fall. I grabbed for my face and he tried to reach for the door knob, but I grabbed at his hand again. He grabbed me by the wrist and twisted my wrist with what seemed like forever, the wrist he has already broken before and I feared he would break it again. We started arguing back and forth exchanging hateful words. He let my wrist go and we tussled back and forth, but he finally pulled the door open, he shoved me out of the way and made his way out.

"You stupid hoe, you always starting stuff. You can never let me leave in peace. I 'll be back later, and have my dinner cooked. If you want me to stay home, lose some weight and step up your sex game." He yelled as he walked down the stairs to go to the car.

"I hate you Brian, I hate you Brian! I can't stand you, I can't stand you" I screamed as I watched him get into my car and drive away.

I was at a loss of words. I walked back into the apartment and closed the door and BJ was just staring at me.

A minute ago, I forgot all about BJ, all I saw was red. These arguments brought back bad memories of how my parents use to argue.

 I found myself in my mother's shoes, she used to argue with my dad about the same thing and here I was in a relationship with my "dad". Just like my mom, I couldn't keep Brian home because whatever he wanted outside, kept him going back.

I sat back on the couch trying to withhold my tears like nothing happened. BJ crawled into my lap and the tears started flowing like a leaky faucet, they wouldn't stop. I just knew BJ would bring us closer, but things have only gotten worst. BJ fell asleep in my lap and I went and laid him down in his bed. I went into the kitchen to grab a beer to help drown out my pain. I went from one beer to four beers as I sat on the couch fussing at this imaginary Brian, I made up in my mind.

In the middle of me arguing with imaginary Brian, I hear my phone ringing from the bedroom. I stumbled into the room grabbed the phone and laid across the bed. I was drunk.

"Helloooo." I answered slurring my words.

"What you are doing girl?" Shantel asked.

"Nothing, girl, over here drunk."

"By, yourself?"

I started laughing "Yeaaaaaa, girl by myself. You know that nigga ain't never here."

"Well, speaking of Brian, you know you my sis and I love you to death. I hate to tell you this, but I wouldn't be a real friend if I didn't. I'm over here at *Wal-Mart* and I see Brian up in here with some old' ugly whore, she tore down girl."

My heart sank. I started sobbing into the phone. No, No! Shan come get me please! Please come get me."

"And to top it off Joy, she had a pregnancy test in her hand." Shantel said angrily into the phone. "I'm so sorry Joy."

My body tensed up, my jaw tightened. I screamed into the phone. "He got a hoe pregnant? He got a hoe pregnant, after he told me he didn't want any more kids, after he been pulling out every time when we have sex!"

"Shan!" I yelled into the phone.

"No! No! No! No!" I screamed into the phone. I started crying again.

"Joy? Joy?" Shantel called for me, but I couldn't answer back. I was in shock and distraught. I was going through so many emotions all in a short span of time. I finally replied.

"Let me call you back." I said into the phone and then I hung up.

She called back several times, but I didn't answer. I called Brian and he sent me to voicemail all twenty-eight times; My mind was racing. I started pacing back and forth across the bedroom floor trying to make sense of what I just heard. Brian has done many of things, but this here takes the cake. He was trying to start a family with another woman, he was trying to give her what was mine. Rage and anger began to set in.

My eyes scanned the room for something of his I could destroy; I locked my eyes on his clothes. I pulled every shirt and pants he owned off the hanger and pulled out a few pairs of his shoes. I carried as many as I could to the bathroom and put them inside the tub. I went back and grabbed the rest of his belongings until the tub was full. I went into the kitchen and grabbed the bleach from underneath the kitchen sink. The gallon was half full and I poured all of it onto his clothes.

I grabbed some of BJ's baby powder and I sprinkled some onto the clothes. I went back into the kitchen and grabbed several condiments out of the refrigerator and dumped them all on his clothes until I felt satisfied with the damage. I turned the water on and allowed his items to get soaked. I went and grabbed another beer and I popped it opened and sat next to the tub. I went through a bunch of emotions; I was sad, I was angry, I was distraught, I was enraged and I wanted to destroy more of his things but I couldn't find the strength to move.

I didn't know how to feel anymore, I felt dead on the inside. This was real hell on earth, I was living in hell. I leaned my head over and it rested on the tub and I wept until my head felt like it was going to burst. I wanted this pain to go away, and now I could see why my mom left the way she did. She wanted to get out of her hell on earth and I'm thinking about leaving the way she did.

Chapter 20

"Where Home Is"

"Go Grab, your shoes!" I yell at BJ.

Shantel was having a surprise cook-out for Desmond and BJ and I was already forty-five minutes late because I had to fight with Brian just to use my car to go. We argued the whole morning about it and he decided that he would drop me off and that Shantel would bring me back home. I agreed to that arrangement just so I could go. Brian was invited, but he declined like always, so I was going alone.

"BJ go grab your shoes, now!" I yelled at him again as I applied a little bit of lip-gloss onto my lips.

It was the beginning of Summer 2010 and the weather was warming up quite nice. I had selected a nice halter top dress to wear, but since Brian declined to go, I had to choose another "Brian Approved" Outfit that was appropriate to wear since he wasn't going to be around. I decided to wear some blue jeans capris with a red and blue striped short-sleeve shirt and some red flip flops. I looked simple, but I knew this outfit would minimize the arguments.

Brian and I were still having problems on top of problems.

After I destroyed all his things he was beyond pissed; we got into a bad physical fight when he came home and saw his things floating in the tub. Even though I ended up with a bloody nose and a busted lip, I didn't have any remorse about destroying his things. I was satisfied, until one of his little girls bought him a couple pairs of clothes. I wanted to set those on fire but, I didn't have the energy to fight with him, better her money than mine.

He was still drinking like there was no tomorrow and it was out of control. He would drink for breakfast, lunch and dinner. The little money we did have went to his drinking and if it wasn't for me working part-time at Taco Bell, the Work First assistance I was getting and staying in Public housing, we would be worse off than we already were. No matter how good I cooked or cleaned or how obedient I was to Brian, I just couldn't get Brian to do right. He was just like my daddy.

I had bouts of depression, he made me feel like I wasn't good enough and there were days I wanted to give up on life completely, but I fought through because he always found his way back home and I really did love him.

I didn't want to lose; I couldn't let another woman take him from me. Even after finding the ultrasound picture in his drawer confirming he had another woman pregnant, I refused to let her win. I was devastated about the pregnancy but, I couldn't let him go, she wasn't about to have the family I built. So, I dealt with it, her and the baby for the sake of trying to keep my family together.

We pulled out the worst in one another and we were always fighting verbally and physically. We exposed B.J to all of it, as much as I wanted all the pain to end, I just didn't have the strength to leave Brian, I knew no one would love me like he did and B.J needed his daddy.

We finally arrived at Shantel's townhouse. Brian dropped me off and he didn't even go in to speak; He sped off, probably rushing to lay up somewhere. BJ and I walked up to the door and I could hear the music blasting through the door. I knock on the door and her daughter Aaliyah opened the door.

"What are you doing opening the door?" I said.

"My mommy told me to." She said.

Aaliyah was about five years old and she looked just like her daddy, but she was tall and slim like Shantel. She was a pretty little thing.

"Ima get her." I said as I leaned in to give her a hug and kiss.

"Hey, BJ, come here." she said as she took him by the hand and led him towards the back of the house.

"Be good, BJ!" I yell out.

I walked through the living room and it seemed like all the adults were outside. I opened the patio door and stepped outside; I could smell the burgers cooking on the grill.

The music was just right. It was a lot of people out there. I spoke to a few people I recognized before I made my way over to Shantel.

"Well, look who finally showed up." Shantel said jokingly.

"Girl, my bad, I'll tell you about that later." I said bending over to give her a hug. She looked nice. She was about four months pregnant with their third child. She had that pregnancy glow.

"Where's Brian?" she asked.

"Girl, that's why we late and you know how he be acting, he said he wasn't coming."

She rolled her eyes. "Whatever, forget him too, anyway, if you want a beer or something there's some in the cooler and if you're hungry go fix you a plate, we got a lot of food."

I walked over to the cooler and grabbed me a beer and fixed me a plate and sat in the chair near Shantel as she played Spades with Desmond, Desmond's sister Ranell and her boyfriend.

"Where Brian at?" Desmond asked

I shrugged my shoulders. "He out somewhere." I was slightly embarrassed to answer.

"You know how ya'll boys do" Shantel interjected hi-fiving Ranell. All the women started laughing.

"Don't even start, we don't be doing nothing." Desmond said.

Shantel paused the Spades game. She responded with a little attitude. "You know how ya'll can't stay faithful."

You could see Desmond's face tense up. He looked like he was getting upset.

"Shantel, we not about to do this right now." Desmond said.

"I'm just saying y'all dudes ain't right." She said.

"And y'all chicks ain't either, old scandalous women." Desmond said.

"Oh, here you go." Shantel replied.

They started arguing back and forth, they were never afraid of having an audience. Curse words flew back and forth and it seemed like some unresolved issues were coming forward. Shantel and Desmond have been together since she was fifteen.
They had just as much drama as me and Brian, except he wasn't hitting on her and he kept a job.
Shantel has put up with so much stuff, other women, outside pregnancies, STD's, Desmond getting locked up and the list goes on.

Shantel wasn't going anywhere and neither was Desmond. He was always there for her when it mattered most, that was something I always envied about their relationship.

Ranell and her boyfriend ended up getting them to calm down. They kissed it out and went back to playing spades. In the mist of them arguing, I made my way back to the food table to grab some more ribs.

"What's up Joy?" A familiar voice said from behind.

I turned around and my stomach dropped. There stood Jamier oozing with fineness. Even after all these years he still looked good. I stopped fixing my plate.

"Hey." I said trying not to seem nervous, but I was; he was so fine. We exchanged hugs and he smelled so good, I could've melted in his arms.

"So, how have you been?" He asked.

"I've been O.K., what about you?"

"I'm doing well, you still got you a man?"

I chuckled. "Yea I still have me a man."

"But are you happy?" He asked.

"I mean we're good. Like most relationships we have our problems, but I love him though."

"Dang, man. You need to let him go. I've been thinking about you since the last time I saw you at the club all those years ago. I've been trying to get with you. You need to come back home and stop playing."

I laughed even harder and cut my eyes at him. "Yea, O.K., so you can break my heart again?"

"You can't hold me to my past, Ima changed man." he said.

"Yea, Yea that's what they all say." I said rolling my neck at him.

He grabbed my hand. "Let's hang out tonight, we could get a room." He flashed those pretty white teeth and I almost fell right into temptation. I pulled my hand away.

"I can't do that." I said shaking my head. "My man doesn't play and I ain't got time for that and you probably got some chick back in Atlanta."

"Naw, I told you, I've changed. I don't have anybody. And can't nobody make me feel like you?" He said laughing a bit.

I gave him a smirk. *"Fine as he is, yeah right."* I thought to myself.

"Umhmm, I hear you Jamier."

We stood near the food table and talked a little bit more. After college, he didn't make it to the pros; He went overseas and played for a couple of years. It wasn't satisfying him so he moved back and found a Human Resource Position at a firm in Atlanta. He didn't have any children. He was doing well which made me realize how bad off I was with Brian.

We decided to play spades with Desmond and Shantel; It felt like the good old days. We laughed, joked and we even played a few drinking games. Jamier kept trying to get me to leave with him and as tempting as it was, I couldn't do that to Brian, even though I missed the fun I use to have with Jamier. Brian and I had so much drama that we barely did anything fun and I wanted to feel that again.

It was good seeing Jamier and escaping my reality for a few hours and now I was glad that Brian didn't come. Brian called me and told me it was time for me to get home, so I asked Shantel if she could take me home. I packed up a few plates, got BJ ready and we made our way to Shantel's truck.

On the ride, home I couldn't help but think about Jamier and how my life would be if I had stayed with him and never met Brain. I couldn't get him off my mind, I missed his smile and how much fun we had together.

"Jamier was looking good wasn't he girl." Shantel inquired.

"Girl, yes and if I wasn't with Brian, I would've went to that hotel with him. I got turned on looking at him, we had so much fun."

"I know, reminded me of the old days. I miss ya'll together." Shantel said.

"Why did I have to meet Brian?" I said laughing.

"I know right!" Shantel responded in agreeance.

Brian called interrupting my conversation with Shantel.

"Hello." I said into the phone.

"Where you at with my son?"

"Your son, really? Well we're on the way home."

"You better be on your way."

"We are I promise, Brian."

He hung up the phone. I went from cloud nine to hell in 0.5 seconds. My thoughts went straight to how much Brian got on my nerves and how I dreaded going home. Shantel and I talked a little bit more and then we pulled into my apartment complex. I kissed her good-bye, grabbed BJ and the bags of food out of her car. I tiredly walked up the stairs wishing I was going home to Jamier.

"Out of all the nights he wants to come home early. Why did it have to be tonight?" I thought to myself as I noticed my car parked in the parking lot.

I slid my key into the door and to my surprise Brian wasn't there. It was quiet in the apartment and now I was wondering where Brian was and who picked him up. I lay BJ down on the couch and I put away the food in the kitchen. I was a little tipsy, so I grabbed some water and my mind went back to Jamier.

"Dang I miss him." I thought as I swallowed a drink of water.

I picked BJ up and carried him into his room and kissed him on his cheek put him to bed and made my way to my room. I turned on the bedroom light and I noticed Brian was already asleep in the bed. I quickly turned the light off trying not to wake him. I crept over to the bathroom, I slipped off my clothes and took a hot shower. My mind kept wondering about Jamier and I wished he was standing in the shower with me.

I dried off, applied my lotion, put on my night gown and climbed in the bed. I kept reminiscing about Jamier and I wished he was here instead of Brian. I felt Brian turnover and he grabbed me and snuggled up behind me.

He put his hands between my legs and started messing with my vagina. I could feel his kisses on my neck. I was completely turned off because he interrupted my thoughts about Jamier. I was annoyed and I just wanted to go to sleep in peace.

He turned me over, climbed on top of me and we had sex, but this time it felt so different; He took his time. He was kissing me and kept telling me he loved me. We hadn't made love like this in a few months. Every thought I had about Jamier vanished as I made love to Brian. In this very moment, I knew why I stayed. I don't know what got into Brian tonight, but I liked it; we made love until the sun came up. Brian truly did love me; he was just depressed. He just needed to get back on track and then we would be good. He was just being a man and sometimes you should let your man be a man. He knew where home was even if he strayed on occasions and I knew home was right here with Brian.

Chapter 21

"How Can I live without You"

I woke up the next morning in awe of last night. Brian and I haven't connected like that in a long time. The sex we've been having over the past few months was quick, straight to the point and it lacked foreplay and emotion; I was really taken back by it. I hear laughter coming from the living room; Something was cracking BJ up. I slid out of bed to see what was going on. I walked into the living room and Brian was tickling BJ, he was having so much fun. I loved seeing them together. BJ loved his daddy and seeing Brian in his daddy role made me smile. I locked eyes with Brian and we shared a smile.

"Hey babe, ya'll want some breakfast?" I asked as I walked into the kitchen.

"Naw, I'm good. You can grab B.J some cereal and can you pass me a beer."

"Really, Brian a beer?" I thought to myself but because last night went so great, I didn't bother him about it and just grabbed him one out of the refrigerator.

I grabbed the milk, a bowl and the cereal from out of the pantry. I poured BJ a bowl and set it at the table for him.

"BJ, come on BJ!" I yelled into the living room.

Brian carried BJ into the kitchen and sat him down in his booster seat.

"Eat up." He said and walked out of the kitchen.

I cleaned up the milk, put the cereal back in the pantry, went into the living room and sat next to Brian. I handed him his beer and leaned in and kissed him, but he didn't kiss me back. He was acting cold again.

"Everything ok?" I asked as he popped open his beer. He took a few sips.

"Naw, I got something to talk to you about." He said still drinking his beer.

"What's up Brian? What is it? Is it serious?"

"Yeah." He said looking away.

My heart started beating fast. I didn't know what he wanted to talk about, but I was going to find out.

"Brian, don't tell me Monique pregnant again. Brian, you said you was done with her and you were just there for Melina, are you still sleeping with her?" I yelled.

"Naw, I ain't sleeping with Monique, I already told you that." He replied.

"So, what is it then?" I said with a confused look plastered on my face.

He stood up. "Joy, I met someone else, and I'm going to be with her. She makes me feel good, and I can't keep living like this. I keep lying to her and I don't want to lie to her anymore. She trying to help with my drinking. She loves me and I love her too."

The life I had with Brian came crashing down right before my eyes. The tears rushed from my eyes like a dam spilling over. My throat closed and I was gasping for air; I couldn't breathe. My heart was being ripped from my chest. I sat there rocking back and forth trying to make sense of what I just heard.

"You are doing what?" I asked trying to catch my breath.

"I'm done with you. I don't love you like I use to. It ain't been the same for years and I stayed because of BJ. I'm tired of you, you did nothing but bring me down. You messed my life up, you got me drinking again, I can't do it anymore. I hate I met you." He said.

"So, that's it? After everything I put up with? After all the black eyes, busted lips, STDs and other women, you're done with me? Brian, I love you and I tried to help you. I tried to be there for you, but you wanted to do your own thing. Messed up your life? You destroyed me and my life. I messed up your life, really? I messed up your life! Tell me how!" I screamed and with every word the tears kept falling.

"It's over, Joy. I'll be there for B.J." he said nonchalantly walking towards the door. I followed behind him yelling.

"Just forget about me, and our family. Brian, I did everything for you. Let you keep me locked up in this house, let you control what I wore, who I talked to, my friends. I cooked and cleaned for you and I can't believe you love someone else. You are leaving me for someone else, after everything. I gave you all of me, all of me and this is how you do me, really?" The tears wouldn't stop.

"After, everything!" I screamed. I mushed him in the back of the head. He turned around and we tussled back and forth. He threw me back on the couch. I stood up and walked over towards him, but I kept my distance, so I could get answers.

"So, what was last night about? You just told me you loved me last night, what was that about?" I asked the tears still falling from my eyes.

"I got caught in the moment. I have love for you, but I don't love you anymore. I haven't for a while." He walked backed towards the door.

"You don't love me anymore Brian? After everything Brian, you don't love me." My voice was shaky and I couldn't stop crying if I tried.

My heart felt like it was ran over by an eighteen-wheeler truck. I was having a hard time breathing again.

"No!" I gasped for air. "No!" I screamed gasping for air. I fell at his feet hysterically crying. "You can't leave me, you can't go. I can be better, tell me what I got to do, and I'll do it. Brian don't leave me, I need you. Please stay, don't go. If you leave me, who's going to love me? Please don't go!"

"Joy, get the hell up. I can't do this anymore. I'm done, deal with it." He said cold. He had no empathy for my feelings.

I reached for his pants and tried to pull them down so I could perform oral sex on him, but he pushed my head away.

"Get up, Joy. Stop acting stupid, let me go!" He yelled.

"I can be everything you need. Brian, I can do better than her. Just tell me what I need to do. I don't care about the other women, you could have them just don't leave me." I put my head in my hands and I wept and wept.

"Bye, Joy." He threw my car keys towards me. I heard the door open and then the door closed; I knew he was gone.

I sat in that spot on my knees for forever and I cried and cried and then I was mad, then I was sad, then I was angry again, I went through a cycle of different emotions trying to make sense of Brian's confession. Brian and I had some issues, but I would've never thought Brian would leave me for another woman.

"Mommy, Mommy!" I heard BJ screaming from the kitchen as I realized I left him in there to eat. I dragged myself into the kitchen and I took him out his booster seat. I couldn't focus on BJ right now, so I pulled out some of his toys and told him to go play. I searched for my cell phone and found it on the nightstand in the bedroom. I laid across the bed and dialed Brian's number. He sent me straight to voicemail. I called about 54 times within five minutes and all my calls were ignored.

Misery began to set in and I got lost in my own thoughts; I realized another man has left me.

I don't know what it was about me that made people want to leave me. I guess I just wasn't lovable. Who would love me? I was ugly, fat, I use to strip and have sex for money. I couldn't stay pregnant and I killed four of my own babies. I was useless and I wasn't good for nothing. I was the worst person ever and I just wasn't good enough. All the men I've been with left me in some way, shape or form for some other woman, who probably was better than me; I sucked.

Why couldn't I keep Brian happy? If I would have done that, he would still be here, but I was too messed up for him, and I messed up his life. Maybe he was right, he's better off without me. I'm not good for anyone, why am I still here? Why should I live?

I picked myself up off the bed and went into the kitchen in search of something to ease my pain. I remembered we had a bottle of Gin in the cabinet. I grabbed the Gin out of the cabinet, it was half full. I took it straight and finished the bottle. I walked back over to refrigerator and grabbed a couple of beers. I noticed the butcher knife and I grabbed that too. I walked over to the kitchen table and found myself a seat. In between sips of beer, I contemplated taking my own life. I had no life without Brian, he was the only one who knew the real me and if he didn't want me, I know no one else would. Who really needed me to be around? No one needed me. I started playing around with the knife. I put it up to my wrist and thought about cutting myself, but then I thought slitting my throat would make me die faster.

I called Brian a couple more times and again he sent me straight to voicemail. I decided to leave him message.

"I HATE YOU! You are so stupid! Why did you leave me like this and for some chick? For some chick, Brian? I gave you all of me and you do me this WAYYYYYYYYYYY! I hate you and now I don't know how I'm going to live without you. What am I supposed to do without you? I need YOUUUUUUUU! I love you so much Brian, I just want our family back together. I can love you for real, please come back to me!" I screamed into the phone.

I slammed the phone down, it hit the table and fell on the floor. I didn't bother to pick it up. I picked up the knife and put it up to my neck. I could feel the cold blade as it rested on my neck. I pushed it closer to my neck and I was ready to go. I no longer wanted to live. The tears came pouring down from my eyes, but I was ready. I was ready to die. I went to pull at the knife and BJ runs in the kitchen. I put the knife down.

"Mommy, look at my car, it's blue." He said as he pushes his car in my face.

"That's nice, BJ. It's a cool car." I said.

"Mommy, why you are crying?" He asked.

"Mommy's ok, I'm just a little sad"

"Don't be sad mommy, I love you." He said as he kissed me on my cheek and ran out of the kitchen.

I almost did it. If BJ hadn't run into the kitchen, I would've killed myself. I loved that little boy, but the pain I felt was beyond him. I know he loved me but there was another kind of love that I longed for and I so desperately needed. Life just didn't feel worth living if I couldn't feel that love. My feelings were all over the place, I started thinking about my mother and her suicide; now I was re-living her life. I love a man who doesn't love me. Brian abandoned me just like my daddy did my mother. I look at the knife sitting on the table and part of me wanted to pick it up again, but a part of me couldn't because of BJ.

I finished up the last bottle of beer and stood up from the table. I could barely stand, I could feel the alcohol kicking in. I stumbled over to the couch and laid myself across the sofa and cried myself to sleep.

Chapter 22

"The best way to get over an Old man is to Get under a new One."

"Shantel, you almost ready to go?" I said with a little irritation in my voice.

"I'm ready, I'm ready." She said as she walked into her living room waddling, wearing a homemade bun in the oven costume.

She was about seven months pregnant. It was Halloween and we were on our way to take the children trick or treating at the mall. I didn't have the energy to dress up, but BJ was Spiderman and he was excited. I really wanted to stay home, after everything I've been through the last few months. I wasn't feeling it, but Shantel dragged me out of the house saying I should do it for BJ; So here I am. We loaded the children in the car and to the mall we went.

After Brian left, I was a complete wreck. The man I loved and the father of my son left me to raise our son alone; I died on the inside. Even though there were times I wanted to be done with Brian, I was never prepared for this. It hurts today just as much as it did the day he left.

I slipped into a deep depression. I wouldn't eat, I could barely sleep and all I wanted to do was lay around and cry. Some days I had to force myself out of bed to feed BJ and on some days, he only ate once. I barely interacted with BJ, when he wanted to play. I would tell him to play by himself and I would just lay on the couch lifeless.

There were no baths, I just laid around in my own filth and BJ did the same. I called Brian three days straight after he left. I probably called him from the time I woke up until the late evening. He would never answer, so I left several voicemails trying to convince him to come back; some voicemails were cussing him out for leaving me. When I tried to call on the fourth day, he had changed his number and blocked me on Facebook. I shut out the world even Shantel, I didn't want to deal with anyone. I had thoughts of suicide on several occasions, especially when I was extremely sad and down. I pitied myself and blamed myself for Brian leaving me, but every time I was close to doing it, thoughts of BJ flashed in my head; I just couldn't go through with it.

About two weeks after Brian left, Shantel came by to check on me after my manager Ms. Mary was worried about me because it was unusual for me not to show up for any of my shifts.

When she came by we talked and I confessed everything to her. She convinced me to move in with her. She said she was worried about me and wanted to help me out with BJ; A week later BJ and I was living with her. I didn't give my housing any notice, I just left. I didn't want to stay there anyway, it reminded me of Brian.

I was grateful that she was willing to help me out, but living with her didn't make me feel any better. I started to hate seeing her and Desmond interact. They had something I longed for and to see them kiss made me sick to my stomach. I stayed up in the room for the most part and I asked Shantel to give me time to work through everything. She respected that and gave me my space, she took care of BJ like he was her own son.

The more and more I stayed in the room the depressed I got; my emotions were up and down. I did want to feel better, but Brian did a number on me. I just wanted to be loved, I just wanted to be happy and I just wanted to feel needed. Ever since I was younger, I felt pushed to the side, I felt like people just didn't care about me. My mother, my dad, my grandparents, and the different men, they all abandoned me. I wasn't worth keeping, I wasn't worth loving, they all left me. I didn't want to feel this way, but I couldn't shake this. I couldn't understand why, why me? While I should feel a sense of relief, I couldn't help but feel broken and discarded. My mother had the nerve to name me Joy, but real joy was something I never felt.

"Did you hear me?" Shantel said interrupting my thoughts.

"Naw, my bad. What did you say?"

"I said, Jamier has been asking about you since the cook-out."

"Asking about what?" I inquired.

"You. He said he wants to get with you and he asked me were you still with Brian."

"What did you say?"

"I told him, you weren't. So now he really trying to get with you."

"Shan, I don't know. I ain't really trying to be with nobody, I'm still in love with Brian."

"I know Joy, but they say the best way to get over your old guy is to get under a new one. It beats you staying stuck up in your room. I miss the old you, when you're happy and in love."

"Yea, but he all the way in Atlanta, I ain't doing long distance."

"Naw, he moved back home about a month and a half ago. His mother got real sick and he came back to help his dad take care of her. So, he's here and ya'll could get together."

"Um, ok. I'll think about it."

"Joy, give him another chance. He really wants you and you are all he talks about. I'm tired of seeing you crying over Brian, move on with Jamier."

"Shan, I don't want nothing serious. I just can't give everything to a man again."

"You ain't got to be his girl. Ya'll could just kick it, maybe have sex, I'm tired of you focusing on Brian, focus on Jamier and have some fun." She said laughing.

"I'll think about it!!"

"Please do, so you can let go of Brian and move on. I'll text you his number"

We made it to the mall. We planned on taking the children store to store. I couldn't help, but think that maybe Shantel was right, Jamier could be the one to help me move on from Brian. I'm tired of crying and maybe I could have some fun with Jamier, nothing too serious.
We went to as many stores as we could to make sure the children got enough candy. BJ had so much fun, he really became Spiderman when people would complement his costume. Shantel really knew what to do to bring my spirits up and I loved her for that. I hadn't been out in months and I was glad I came; seeing BJ happy made me feel good. Maybe I'll give Jamier a call tomorrow.

I woke up the next morning feeling a little better than I had in a while. I woke up with Jamier on my brain. I had a lot of love for him and even though he did his fair share of dirt, we were older now and people can change. I sat at the edge of my bed, and grabbed my cell phone to call Jamier and for some reason I was nervous.

"Hello." he said into the phone.

"Hey, Jamier." I said softly into the phone.

"Who is this?" he asked.

"Um, it's Joy."

"Yo, what's up? How are you doing?"

"I'm, ok. Shan said you've been asking about me."

"Yea, after seeing you again at the cook-out, I've been trying to get back in contact with you. What you are doing tonight?" He asked.

"Nothing, just sitting around the house."

"You want to get together tonight? Let's kick it like old times." He said laughing into the phone.

"I guess we can."

"Everything good Joy?"

"Yea, I just been sad lately, trying to get over my ex."

"Well come out with me, I'll make you forget about that dude." He said confidently.

"Ok, I'll be ready."

"Be ready at nine. You still staying over at Des' house."

"Yea, so pick me up here."

"Alright, cool. I'll text you when I'm on the way. Let me get off this phone and back to work. Talk to you later."

"Ok, see you later."

A feeling of excitement came over me, something I haven't felt in a long time. Jamier just did something to me and I was ready to see him.

I get out of bed and I woke BJ up to start our day. I go downstairs to make him breakfast and afterwards we hung out with Shantel and her son DJ while Aaliyah was off at school. We ran around to a few stores and we made it back with enough time for me to get ready for my date with Jamier. Shantel was so excited, she's been wanting us to be a foursome again for years and maybe she'll get her wish.

Getting ready for tonight was a struggle. I had lost a lot of weight during my depression and I just didn't feel pretty. I almost cancelled the date; I was frustrated because I couldn't find an outfit I looked decent in. Shantel finally gave me a white turtleneck sweater and I paired it with my black leggings and my knee-high boots with the heels. It wasn't the best-looking outfit, but it made due. My hair was shorter than it used to be because I had to cut off a lot of the damage where it was matted, so it fell a little past my ears. I flat ironed it and shaped it to look like a bob.

I gave myself another look over in the mirror, and I didn't look as good as I wanted, but maybe he'll like it. I applied some lip gloss, sprayed on some perfume and went downstairs to wait for him to arrive.

Jamier arrived about 9:30p and he texted me to let me know he was outside. I kissed BJ goodbye, let Shan know I was leaving, grabbed my coat and I dashed out the door. When I opened the car door, all the old feelings I had for him came rushing back. He was looking good and his facial hair took his fineness to another level. I slid into the passenger seat. I couldn't really get a peep of what he was wearing but I know he was fly. He was always a good dresser. Jamier had a new ride, it was an all-white s550 *Mercedes Benz*. Jamier always had great taste and it felt good to be in his presence.

We decided to do dinner at *Chili's*. Even though I wasn't a big fan of chain restaurants, I hadn't been to one in so long, I was happy to be out. The restaurant was a little packed for it to be a Wednesday. We waited about fifteen minutes for our table. We were finally seated and the conversation just flowed.

"I can't believe, I'm here with you." I said.

"I know right." He replied.

"I never thought, well you know after everything we've been through that you and I would connect again." I said.

"Well, I told you, I'm different now and every time I see you it brings back old memories."

"Old memories like what?" I inquired.

"I don't want to say it." He said acting coy.

"Naw, tell me."

"You were a good girl back then and I messed up. Every time I see you I can't help but think about how good sex was with you. Nobody has ever made me feel like you did."

"What, really the sex? You miss the sex?" I said smirking.

"I miss you too. You held me down and we had fun times but you did have some good stuff. Can you blame me?" He said chuckling.

I hadn't heard a compliment in so long it felt good to hear Jamier talk about me and my sex in a good way. Brian said my sex was trash and I needed to step it up, but Jamier loved it and that made me smile.

"Same Old Jamier." I said laughing.

"You know you miss this too." He said rubbing his beard.

I rolled my eyes at him jokingly. "Whatever!"

The waitress came over and interrupted our
conversation to get our orders. Once our orders were
placed we jumped back into our conversation.

"So, what are you looking for, a relationship?" I asked
Jamier.

"Naw, with everything going on with my mom, I
can't dedicate time to a relationship, but I wouldn't
mind just having a friend. You know to kick it with
no strings attached."

"Ok, yeah I don't know if I could do a relationship,
after everything that went down with my ex, I don't
know if I could do that again."

"What went down between ya'll anyway."

"He basically woke up one day and told me he didn't
want to be with me anymore, He left me to go be with
another woman. I put up with so much from him. He
controlled me, he cheated and he abused me and he
had a child on me. Jamier, I went through hell with
him. So, I can't do another relationship right now, but
I can use some fun."

"Oh, wow, that's messed up. I told you to leave that
dude when I saw you at the cook-out."

"Yea, I know but I loved him. I still love him and I
couldn't leave him then. We have a son together and I
wanted to make my family work. He hurt me so bad."
I almost teared up.

"You OK? Don't cry." He said, consoling me.

"I'm sorry Jamier, every time I think about everything he took me through, I get emotional. I'm still not over it."

"That's why I'm here, to take your mind off that dude, he didn't know what he had."

"He sho'll didn't!" I said shaking my head.

"Enough about that dude, you still trying to hang out afterwards."

"Yea, I mean I don't have anything else to do."

"Ok, cool I was going to grab us a hotel, if you want to stay the night with me."

"Yes, I'm down." I said blushing.

We finished up our meal. We laughed and talked about some old memories from high school. We left the restaurant and Jamier decided to grab us a room at the Holiday Inn. I was turned on before we even pulled up. I knew what he wanted when he got us the hotel but I had no problem giving it to him. I wanted to take my mind off Brian and focus on Jamier and I knew this was needed.

Once we were inside the room. Jamier gave me a shot of Patron. I hadn't had a drink since the first few days Brian left me. I had run out of alcohol and I never went to the store to get more.
I threw the shot back and that led us to taking a few more. I was feeling good. He got undressed and climbed in the bed. I took off my leggings and left my turtleneck on and climbed in the bed and snuggled up next to him.
He started kissing me on my neck and we shared a few kisses. It did feel a little weird to be with another man outside of Brian but it felt good to be wanted.

Jamier pulled out a condom and put it on. Which shocked me because he never used condoms.

"Oh, you're protecting yourself." I said laughing.

"I told you, I've changed." He said as he climbed on top of me.

He kissed me on the lips and we made love and I exploded from the inside out and what I've been waiting for finally happened. I was in awe, this felt like old times, tears fell from my eyes. Our connection was something pure and real and I could really tell he missed me. We continued the party for several hours until we both tired out and fell asleep.

Chapter 23

"On to the Next One"

It was about 5:33 in the evening. I was on my way to pick B.J up from daycare. Trey Songz *"Can't be Friends"* was blasting from my speakers; It made me think of Jamier. I picked up my phone and sent him a quick text hoping he would come over tonight.

5:37pm: Hey wyd? Hit me up when you get a chance.

We were four months into the new year and I was finally getting myself together thanks to Jamier and Shantel. After everything that happened with Brian, I told Ms. Mary from Taco Bell that I wasn't coming back, because I had some family issues to work through. She understood and said I would always have a job but I didn't want to work there anymore. Jamier's sister was able to get me a job at her clothing store. I was able to move out of Shantel's place and find BJ and I a one bedroom apartment, in a decent part of town. I still received government assistance in the form of food stamps and a daycare voucher. I was doing O.K. for myself, living alone taking care of B.J.

Brian finally reached out to me and asked if he could see B.J but the conversation didn't go well. I'm still upset about how he left me and I told him I wasn't ready to let him see B.J and whenever I was ready, I would let him know. Brian didn't deserve to see B.J, at least not right now.

My phone vibrated. Jamier had texted me back.

5:40pm Jamier: What's up?

5:41pm Me: Are you coming over tonight?

About five minutes went by and I sent the same text again.

5:46pm Me: Are you coming over tonight??

Two minutes later my phone vibrated.

5:48pm Jameir: Naw, probably not, I'm busy tonight.

I decided to give him a call and he sent me straight to voicemail. I called one more time and again same thing, straight to voicemail. I was starting to get upset, *was he doing that purposely or did his phone die?* I thought to myself.

Things were fun between Jamier and I at the beginning. Our relationship was mainly sexual but I didn't care at first. I was just glad to have him around to help me get over Brian.

The problems came about a month or so ago when I started wanted more from him and more of his time. I believed I could do the no strings attached thing but I couldn't, well not with Jamier because I loved him. Every time I had sex with him it drew me closer to him. I wanted to be with him again but he made it clear that a relationship wasn't what he wanted.

My feelings for him grew and grew and they were only making things worse. I began to nag him and flip out if he didn't call me or if he didn't text me or if we were together and somebody called him. I would catch an attitude with him and then I'll question him about it, and then we would start arguing.

The more my emotions grew, the more he pulled away. After a while I was the one who would initiate the conversation, and when he responded it would be short and dry. We had sex less and less.

"Hello." Shantel said into the phone.

"Shan, can you do me a huge favor? Can you pick B.J up from the daycare? I got to run somewhere really quick and don't know if I'll be there on time."

"Yea, I can. Everything ok?"

"Naw, but I'll fill you in when I see you."

"Alright, see you later." She said as we hung up the phone.

Jamier's been acting funny towards me and I was tired of it. I made up in my mind that I was going to confront him and get some answers. I was going to ride over his place to see what was up. I had no clue if he was home or not but I was about to take a chance and see. I pulled into his apt complex and it must've been my lucky day because his car was parked in his parking space. I found an empty space a few spots down from Jamier's car and I pulled in.

I got out of the car and I still had on my work clothes and I looked a mess but I was on a mission, so I didn't care. I walked up the stairs nervous and bold at the same time. I clearly wasn't thinking straight but this had to be done. I knocked on the door and Jamier opened the door.

"What are you doing here?" He asked.

"I've been calling you and you sent me straight to voicemail, so I figured I'll come over and talk to you, since you can't call me back."

"I've been busy, I told you that when you texted me earlier."

"Yea, but I called you right after and you didn't answer."

"So that mean, pop up at my house? Joy, you still with the drama, I should've never got back involved with you, why would you pop up at my house though."

"All I asked was for you to keep it real with me and you not. You rather act funny."

"You're acting too crazy. I just wanted some fun, but you trying to act like my girl and you know I don't want no relationship. So yea I pulled back, because I could see you getting crazy."

"I can't help that I love you, you came back into my life, you said you want fun, not me you." I yelled.

"Yea, that's what I said fun, but this ain't fun no more. You knew what it was from the start, it was just sex and nothing more."

"Wow really Jamier? Just sex? So, I was just sex to you." Tears filled my eyes.

"What do you want from me? You agreed to this, all we had was sex, Joy. I ain't your man, so you need to chill."

The tears rolled down my cheeks. "I thought you said you had changed. You're the same Old Jamier."

"I did change but I never changed from what we agreed upon, you did. I told you no strings attached and you wanted to get serious. I didn't lead you on, you agreed to this, so don't come over here trying to act like I did this to you, you did this."

"Wow, just like that." I said with sadness as the tears fell from my eyes.

"You're doing the most and I don't want you like that, I don't have time for your drama."

"So, just like that, you're done with me." I said to him.

"We could still be cool but naw we can't kick it like that anymore. Be good, Joy." He said as he stepped back in and closed the door.

A part of me wanted to knock on his door again but I decided against it. I walked back to my car hurt, betrayed. Jamier made it seem like he wanted me back but all he wanted was the sex. When I got in the car, I cried like a baby, I thought Jamier and I was going to get back together and now that I know that's nearly impossible, it broke my heart.

∙∙

A few days after the incident with Jamier. I really needed some time with my girls so they could help me get over Jamier again. I decided we would go get drinks at a local bar. Ms. Ann kept the children for Shan and me. I invited one of my co-workers Bridgette. Shantel and I grabbed a table and about five minutes later, Bridgette walked in.

Bridgette was really short about 5'2 and slim, she was a pretty girl. She was brown skin and she wore her hair in locs. She reminded me of Lauryn Hill. She was a sweet heart. She was also a single mom and when we met in training at work we instantly clicked and she's been my girl ever since.

"Hey boo." I said to Bridgette as we exchanged hugs.

"Bridgette, this is Shantel, Shan this is Bridgette." I said introducing them to one another. They shook hands and Bridgette took her seat.

"How was work today?" I asked Bridgette.

"It was cool today, we weren't that busy. What you do on your off day?" Bridgette replied.

"Girl, nothing got some rest, after all the crying I've been doing lately, like dang where are the good men." I said waving my hands in the air.

We laughed.

"I thought you and Jamier, was kicking it, what happened with him?" Bridgette asked.

"Girl, so you know we was kicking it right and I'd admit I did start catching feelings but I thought he felt the same way, because of the way he acted when we would have sex, but anyway to make a long story short, he basically said he can't deal with me like that anymore because I want more than he wants to give me."

"Dang, girl he said it like that?" Bridgette asked.

"Basically." I responded.

"He was a cutie though." Bridgette said.

"Yes, he was girl and the sex was so good. Ima miss him though, I just hate I let him back in, and I got played again." I said with a sad face.

"I just knew ya'll would get back together, I was hoping for ya'll." Shantel said.

I shook my head. "Me too."

"Well, forget him. You can do better anyway, on to the next one! Have you ever thought about online dating?" Bridgette said.

"Oh, hell naw! It be to many crazy creeps online." I responded. Shantel and I shared a look of disgust.

"Naw, not everybody online is a creep. I've met some cool dudes online. You should try it, it wouldn't hurt." Bridgette said.

"I don't know about that." I responded.

"Try it, it's this site called *Tagged*, it's almost like *Facebook* but you connect with guys better. We can set you up an account. I met my boo Quan up there." Bridgette told us.

I look over at Shantel and her face said don't do it but what could it hurt, just more ways to meet men. I needed a new boo anyway if I wanted to get over Jamier.

"I guess, I can try it, where do I sign up." I asked Bridgette.

"Yay!" Bridgette said clapping her hands.

"You really going to do it Joy?" Shantel asked.

"What could it hurt? I'ma try it and if I don't like it, I'll delete my account."

Over drinks Bridgette helped me set up my account. We put a couple pictures of me on my page and as soon as it was activated the messages started rolling in. I know Shantel had her reservations but like Bridgette said it was on to the next one, no need to sweat Jamier, I'll just get another man.

Chapter 23

"Tag, You're It"

It's been a few days since I had drinks with my girls and I was grateful to Bridgette for telling me about Tagged. Ever since I signed up my inbox has been jumping and I was hoping to find someone to have fun with and someone who would eventually love me. I wanted to be in love so bad.

There was this one cutie named Devin who caught my attention. He was dark skin and he favored Usher. He was two years younger than me. We exchanged numbers and our conversation flowed from the beginning. I enjoyed talking to him, he was very mature for his age. We made plans to see each this Friday night.

Friday came. I worked my shift at work and when it was time for me to clock out, I rushed out of there. I was ready to see Devin. Shantel watched B.J for me. I rushed home to get dressed but I was a little nervous about meeting Devin. We did exchange pictures back and forth but it's going to be different meeting him in person. While I was getting dressed he texted me and asked me could I meet him at this specific address because his car battery went dead and he couldn't get it to start.

Although I was a little skeptical, I continued to get dress and I made my way over to see him. I gained most of my weight back, kicking it with Jamier all we did was eat and have sex. I threw on some dark blue jean shorts and a hot pink halter top shirt and some pink flip flops. I pushed my hair into a low ponytail. I looked good enough.

When I arrived at the specific address he texted me it wasn't located on the best part of town which made me nervous and I became a little irritated. I thought about turning around but I really wanted to meet him. I kind of liked him. I texted him to let him know I was here. He texted me back and told me to come up to the apartment. I walked up to the door nervous hoping he looked like his pictures and hoping he liked what he saw.

I knocked on the door and he opened it and to my surprise he was cute, but he did look better in the pictures but I could deal with him. He let me in and my eyes scanned the apartment, it was a little unkept and he was straight from the hood. We sat down on the couch and my heart was beating fast. I was so nervous. He grabbed his smoking supplies and he rolled up a blunt.

"Another smoker." I thought to myself.

He lit it up and I took two hits of it and I told him I was good. Every time I looked at him, the cuter he got.

"You, beautiful." He said in between puffs.

"Thanks." I said.

"You got some sexy lips, can I kiss them."

"I guess." I responded.

His breath smelled like smoke but he was a great kisser. He pushed me back on the couch and we kept kissing. He unbuttoned my shorts and pulled them and my underwear off. He stuck his finger in my vagina and I gasped. He pulled out his penis and he tried to put it in.

"You ain't got no condom?" I asked.

"Naw, I ain't got none, you got one."

"No." I said with my face screwed up.

"I'm good though, trust me you, I ain't got nothing and I'll pull out."

I was already feeling good, he called me beautiful and against my better judgement I let him proceed. We had sex and surprisingly it was amazing. Devin was surely working with something. After we were finished, I put on my shorts and I noticed Devin peeking out the window.

"Why you keep looking out the window?" I asked.

"I'm looking out for my mechanic, he supposed to be on the way."

"Oh, ok, so what you trying to do now?"

"Well, my mechanic, on the way and I don't want your beautiful self, stuck in here while we out there looking at my car, so if you want to head out that'll be cool. Just hit me up when you get home."

"Um, ok, cool, I'll hit you up."

Nothing he said sounded right, but he was so cute and I liked him and his sex was amazing so I decided not to give it much thought. As soon as I got in the car he texted me.

9:17pm Devin: You're so beautiful 2 me…. I think I love you…. Hit me up when you get home.

His text had me blushing. He was super cool and I couldn't wait to see what becomes of him and I.

■■■

It's been about two and a half months since I've met Devin and while sex with him was always good. Dealing with him became more of a hassle than anything. He was full of drama and he had so much drama with him and I found out he was a habitual liar. Two weeks after our first encounter. I received a phone call from his girlfriend. At first, he denied it but then he said they were only together because he needed a place to stay and although that was messed up I didn't care about her.

At this point in my life I wanted what I wanted and that was Devin. He started saying he loved me and I fell for it. Every time we got together to hang out we had to meet at cheap run-down motels, which I always had to pay for because he had no job. He would also ask for money which I would give him. The sex drew me closer to him even with his drama, I couldn't leave him alone. I was in love with him.

Things went south with him and I when he moved back home to North Carolina. He said he was only going to be gone for a little while but that decision became permanent. When he was back home, the phone calls got shorter and I heard from him less and less.

One day I got on *Facebook* and I found out Devin had already moved on and was in another relationship. Devin played me, I was so hurt because I was still sending him money when he was back home because he promised he was coming back to me so we can start our family. He was a liar, I know better next time than to trust a liar. He broke my heart big time and I got nothing out of the deal. Devin didn't want me anymore. I had no choice but to move on.

When I was dealing with Devin, I met another guy named Troy on *Tagged*. Troy and I was talking when I was with Devin but I never took it any further because I was dealing with Devin. Now that Devin was out the picture, I figured why not see how it works with Troy.

Troy was short for a guy and a little thick, I wasn't all that attracted to him physically but he had jokes for days which made me like him. He was about four years older than me. I remembered he inboxed me his number a while back. I decided to give him a call.

"Hello." He said into the phone, his voice was very deep.

"Hey, It's Joy, from *Tagged*."

"What's up beautiful, oh you finally called, what you up to?"

"Nothing really, just finished cooking."

"Where's mine?"

"My bad, babe, I got you next time."

"What you be cooking? Matter of fact, can you even cook, you probably be burning stuff."

"Oh, whatever, I can cook, I'll have to cook for you one day, let you see how I do."

"What are you doing this weekend?"

"Um, I don't know. I have my son, so I'll have to get a babysitter or maybe you can come over my place."

"Yea, just let me know."

My phone beeped. I looked at the screen and it was from a private number.

"Hey Troy, hold on. I have a beep."

"Tell your man to call you back." He said.

"Shut up, Troy, hold on." I laughed.

I put Troy on hold and answered the other line.

"Hello." I said

"Hey, Joy." A familiar voice said into the phone.

"What do you want Brian."

"Yo, I'm just trying to see my son, it's Father's Day weekend. I just want him with me."

"Well, you shouldn't have left us." I snapped into the phone."

"Cut the bull, Joy. I'm just trying to see my son." He said into the phone he seemed a little irritated.

Then I remembered I had Troy on the other line and remembered I needed a babysitter so I could hang out with Troy. I wanted to keep saying no, but I said yes just so I could spend the weekend with Troy.

"I guess Brian, when are you picking him up."

"I'll text you with all the details."

"Yea, ok." I rushed back to the other line to get back to Troy.

"Took you long enough." Troy said with sarcasm.

"My bad, that was my son's dad and he's getting him this weekend. So, I guess that means I'm free after all. We talked a little bit more and agreed to get together Saturday evening.

The days came and gone and Saturday was already upon us. I was off today and I woke up with excitement. I let Brian pick up B.J from Shantel, I wasn't ready to see him. I climbed out of bed and started cleaning the house for tonight.

I put my 2011 mix cd into my Cd player and started dancing around the house to *DJ Khaled and Drake "I'm on One"* followed by a couple more jams.

The sun began to set and I prepared myself for the evening. I started cooking. I made chicken alfredo with fettucine noodles with salad and garlic bread. Time started moving faster than I anticipated and when I looked at the clock it was already a quarter pass seven and Troy was due to arrive about 8:30p. I ran into my bedroom and took a shower. I made sure to shave the necessary parts, I wasn't planning on it but you never know how the night may go.

I stepped out the shower and applied lotion all over my body. Since we were just chilling in my apartment, I wanted to be cute but I didn't want to overdo it.

I threw on a yellow tank top and my good old faithful black leggings. I brushed my hair into a high ponytail.

I walked back into the kitchen to check on the food and I hear a knock at the door, my stomach dropped. I thought I wouldn't be nervous but I was. It was 8:30 on the dot, he was right on time. I nervously opened the door and there Troy stood. He was a little taller than me and he had on a stripped short sleeve button down, some dark blue jeans and some all-white air forces. He looked cute.

"Hey." I said moving aside to let him in.

"Hey beautiful." He said reaching around to hug me. He had big arms. I felt an instant chill down my spine.

"It smells good in here."

"Thanks, you ready to eat." I said walking back into the kitchen. Troy followed behind.

Troy sat down at the table and he looked nice. He wore his hair in a brush cut, he had almond shaped eyes and a nice pair of lips. I had to get myself together. My mind started wondering to what I could do to him. I fixed our plates and we began to eat.

"So, do I look like my pictures?" he asked.

"Yea, you do, do I look like mine." I asked.

"You look better than your pictures."

"Thank you." I said blushing.

"How 's the food?"

"It's straight." He replied.

"Yea whatever, not the way you're eating it up." I said laughing.

We talked a little about our lives. He grew up similar to how I did; He grew up without a dad. He had a daughter who I could tell he loved by the way he talked about her. Troy was winning me over with each word that flowed from his lips.

We finished up dinner and we made our way to the living room to watch a couple of movies. We decided to watch an old movie. I popped *Friday* into the DVD player. We sat really close on the couch as if we've known each other for years. He started rubbing my back and asked if he could give me a massage. I couldn't decline his offer so I stretched out on my couch laying on my stomach. Troy gave me a massage and it felt so good.

The massage led to Troy kissing me on my neck and then down my back. He started rubbing on my butt and then he pulled my leggings down and I couldn't bring myself to stop him. We had sex that night and Troy brought something, I've never felt before. Although he was quicker than some, he still left a lasting impression.

Chapter 24

"On again, Off again"

"Ya'll ready to take some shots!" Shantel yells to Bridgette and me as we prepare to go out for my 26th birthday.

I finished applying my mascara and walked into my kitchen and Shantel handed me and Bridgette our shots.
"Drinks Up, Happy Birthday to my ride or Die, She's 26, She's 26!" Shantel yelled.

We downed our shots and we shared a laugh. Turn the music back up Bridgette. She walked over to my Cellphone and turned the music back up and *ASAP Rocky's "Problems"* came through the speakers. I was dancing around in the mirror. I had a sew-in bob cut with blonde highlights that Bridgette did for me. I wore an all-black sleeveless dress, although it was cold outside, I was going to sacrifice my warmth to be cute.
I gave myself another glance in the mirror, Surprisingly, I looked cute. I grabbed my clutch and phone and took another shot and we were out.
Bridgette decided to drive since she didn't plan on drinking that much.

I slide into the front seat and was on a 100, it was my birthday and I was feeling good until I checked my phone and noticed a text from Troy.

11:45pm Troy: Wyd tonight?

I chose to ignore his text and I kept jamming to the music.

After our first date. Troy and I was inseparable. He started staying over at my place every night. We never officially put a title on what we had but we both acted like we were in a relationship. We didn't go out on dates but I did everything a woman would do for her man. I cooked for him and I gave him sex on the regular. I started to fall in love with him.

I started hinting at a relationship but he would always say he wasn't ready for a relationship and he asked me to just be patient. I tried to be patient but I didn't like not having a title. The more I pushed the distant he started to become. He stopped staying over every day and he would stop by like once or twice a week. I felt like he was playing games with me. I would flip out on him when I felt like he was playing me. I sent him nasty text messages and a few days afterwards he would hit me with the *"he need to fallback"* text which would piss me off even more.

We began an on and off sexual relationship. We'll be on for a couple of months and then we'll be off for a couple of months. Even though we had a little drama we always found our way back to one another. The biggest pain came this year in February when he told me he had to fall back again but this time it was because he met someone else.

I was beyond hurt and whomever she was he must've really liked her to cut ties with me. I cried all night behind that situation.

I tried to move on but then he called me again in April and I guess whatever he had with her didn't last because he was right back trying to kick it with me and I foolishly let him back in and we continued to sleep around for the next couple of months.

Over these past two years I hung on to Troy and it's crazy because we didn't go out on dates. We didn't do anything romantic, but I started to love him and my love for him kept a door opened that I should've closed. He did something the other day that pissed me off and I tried to cut him off before my birthday but now he's texting me again.

I rolled my eyes again at the sight of his text message and as much as I wanted to be strong and not reply, I did.

11:50pm Me: Going out for my bday
11:51pm Troy: With who?
11:54pm Me: Bri and Shan
11:56pm Troy: You always out, you such a party girl. I don't like you going clubbing.
11:56pm Me: Are we together? Last time I checked you said you ain't tryna be my man
11:58pm Troy: Cause you always out partying, I don't want my girl in the club.
12:01am Me: Ok, so if I tell you I'll stop, you ready to be with me?
12:06am Troy: wyd after the club?
12:07am Me: Answer my question

12:08am Troy: Come see me tonight
12:08am Me: oh, so you're going to ignore my question?
12:09am Troy: What question?
12:10am Me: The question about being with me if I stopped clubbing.
12:13am Troy: we'll talk about that later, are you coming over?
12:14am Me: yea, I'll text you when I get out of the club.

Every time I talk to Troy about us getting together he always ignores me or try to change the subject. He pisses me off so bad sometimes.

We arrived at the club. We paid for VIP and skipped the line. Tonight, was about to be so much fun. The DJ was good and he kept us on the dance floor the entire night except when we were getting drinks from the bar. The lights came on inside the club and we knew it was time to go. On our way to the car. I sent Troy a quick text to let him know I was leaving the club.

"I had so much fun." Bridgette said unlocking the car door.

"I grabbed the handled and opened the door. I was a little drunk. "Yes girl, the DJ was on point." I responded.

"Ya'll hungry, we can hit up the *Waffle House.*" Shantel said.

"Yea, let's go out there." Bridgette added.

"Um, Idk ya'll, I ain't really that hungry." I said trying to change their minds so I could get over to Troy.

Bridgette looked at me. "So, what we are doing birthday girl?"

"Ya'll could just take me home. I don't really feel like dealing with those people at the *Waffle House*."

"Well, we could go to *IHOP*." Shantel interjected.

"I'm good ya'll, I'm just ready to get home. Thank ya'll for coming out." I said.

"Alright." Bridgette said as she put the keys into the ignition and she began driving towards my apartment.

When we pulled into my parking space at my apartment. I sent Troy a quick text letting him know that he could come over my place. We talked for a little bit in the car about the night. The good, and the bad. Shantel and Bridgette said their peace, we hugged and kissed and they left to go home.

Before I hopped in the shower. I checked my phone and Troy never responded back, I decided to give him a call but he didn't answer. I began to get a little irritated, I could have still been out with my girls but instead I rushed home for him and now he wasn't answering the phone. I hopped in the shower and once I was done, I put on my night clothes and climbed into my bed. I called Troy again and still no answer. I knew I should have never replied. I shook my head and decided not to give it any more energy and I feel asleep.

I woke up the next morning a little agitated about Troy standing me up. I grabbed my cell phone and noticed. I had two missed calls and two unread messages.

9:36am Troy: My bad. I fell asleep last night.

10:23am Troy: U up?

I decided not to respond to his messages and started my day. I walked into my kitchen to fix me some breakfast when I heard my phone ringing. I looked at it and it was Troy. I sent him straight to voicemail. Then he called again. I ignored him. He called again and I finally answered.

"Hello." I said into the phone trying to sound irritated.

"Oh, so you ignoring me now?"

"Didn't you ignore me last night?"

"I texted you and told you I fell asleep, waiting for you to come out the club. I want to come over this morning. You cooking?"

"I could cook."

"Can I come over?"

As much as I wanted to say no. I agreed to let him come over.

"Yea, you can over."

"Alright, I'll be over in about an hour.

"Ok. Bye."

I got myself together and I also cooked breakfast for me and Troy. He came over and he ate and then we had sex and he claimed he had to run out. When he did things like this I felt used and I wished I would have stuck to my guns and ignored him but for some reason I couldn't. He had me weak. I told myself that I was going to cut him off again and this time I was going to be strong.

Chapter 25

"I want Better"

"Joy, Joy, wake up!" Bridgette yelled while rocking me as she sat on my bed Bridgette came over last night for some girl time and she stayed the night because we were going to her Aunt's Women's Luncheon today.

I finally opened my eyes. "Girl, what time is it?" I asked sitting up.

"It's almost 11:30a and you know we got my aunt thing today."

"Dang, you right, what time it start again?"

"At 1p."

"Oh, shoot let me get up and get dressed. Have you taken your shower?"

"Yea, I've been up for a while, Quan woke me up."

"Ya'll are too cute, ok, well let me get up."

I got out of bed and went to the closet to find something to wear. Bridgette said it would be a casual event. I decided to wear a long sleeve navy blue sweater dress, my tights and my knee boots with the heels. I unwrapped my bob and it still looked good. We got dressed and we headed out to the event.

We pulled up to a community center and I got a little nervous. I've never been to a women's event so I didn't have a clue of what to expect. We walked in and it was decorated nice. There was a table full of finger food and then there were round tables decorated with centerpieces and each chair had a menu,name tag and the order of events in front of it.

The Luncheon was titled *"Restoring your Self-Esteem"*. The Luncheon was running a little late it was me and Bridgette and three other ladies. After a while more and more ladies came in a there was one that looked familiar and I realized it was Cyn my homegirl I used to dance with.

"Cyn! Cyn! Hey girl!." I said trying to get her attention.

"Oh, my goodness! Hey Joy." She said when she noticed it was me.

We hugged for at least three minutes.

"Oh wow, how have you been?" Cyn asked.

"I've been good. What about you?"

"Girl, I've been wonderful, we have to catch up, put your number in my phone so we could catch up."

She hands me her phone. I put my number it her phone and I called myself so I could save her number.

Bridgette walks over. "Joy, I didn't know you knew Cyn?"

"Oh, yea we go way back, we use to work together." I said.

"Bridgette is my baby cousin." Cyn said.

"Oh wow, small world." I said. We shared a laugh.

They made an announcement that we were about to start, we made our way back to our tables and decided we would talk afterwards.

The luncheon went good and made me realize why I should leave Troy alone for good. The different speakers talked about how our low self-esteem and the low value we put on ourselves often keep us tied to unhealthy people. They gave us tips on how to improve our self-esteem and I realized today that I suffered from low self-esteem and I wanted my self-esteem to get better. This luncheon had me thinking about my life and I did want better for myself.

After the luncheon was over Cyn and I talked for a little bit, while Bridgette helped her aunt clean up the community center.

"Girl it's so good seeing you." Cyn said.

"I know, once I left the club, we lost contact."

"I know before you left the club, you were talking to a guy named Brian, are you still with him? Cyn asked.

"Girl, hell no. He put me through hell. We have a son together. Girl the stories I could tell you about that relationship would have you thinking you're reading a book."

"When did you finally leave him?"

"I didn't leave him, he woke up one day and decided he didn't want me or his son and left me high and dry. He messed up my whole life."

"I'm sorry to hear that."

"It's ok, I'm doing better now."

"What have you been up to? It's been about seven years or so."

"I've been good, I left the club a couple months after you. Ray and Chocolate got into it and had a big falling out and Chocolate left and some of the girls went with her. Ray started hiring ghetto, trashy chicks and the club went downhill after that. I stacked my money and I got out. I was still getting paid like we use to until I almost got raped one night, I was able to fight him off but that had me shook."

"Dang, that's crazy and that's what Ray get." I interjected.

"I know, he deserved everything he got. But after that I had a rough couple of years. I started dancing down in Atlanta and I was making good money, until the women at that club set me up and jumped me one night, I ended up in the hospital. I tried to press charges, but they hired lawyers and made up some fake alibi's so the case was dismissed. Anyway, after that I came back here and that's when I met my daughter Janell's dad. He was a good man, but me being young and stupid, I didn't appreciate him and I cheated on him with my son Ryan's dad. Me and my son's father stayed together for about three years and that relationship was horrible. He was Satan's son. After numerous attempts, I finally let him go."

"Girl, I guess we both went through some mess."

"Yes, we did, but girl mine came full circle and I'm at a better place now. One Sunday my mother invited me to her church and the message that Sunday seemed like it was just for me. It's like God himself was talking directly to me. I left church that day, feeling different but it wasn't until my mother church's conference where I gave my life to God and my life hasn't been the same. He cleaned me up and made me new. I learned how to love myself.

I met some women who mentored me and taught me how to heal and how to grow. When the time was right, I met a God-fearing man, we got married two years ago and I just gave birth to a baby boy. These past few years have been the best years of my life and it's all because God changed me."

"Cyn, I can really see a difference, you even dress different and talk different. I wonder if I'll be that happy. The guy I'm dealing with right now, we be on and then we be off, I'm tired of dealing with him. I want a good man but it seems like I'll never find one." I said.

"I used to think like you but then I learned that it's all about what we require, it's good men out here, you just have to believe it. We need to get together one weekend, so we can really talk. Maybe one day you'll come to my church."

"I don't know about that, I don't really do church. I haven't been since I was a kid." I said.

"Oh ok, well maybe we can have a girl's night or something like that. I 'll text you."

"Ok cool." I said giving her a hug.

"See you soon." Cyn said.

Bridgette and her aunt was finally done cleaning up. We hopped in the car. We talked a little bit about the luncheon.

She dropped me off at home. I had a lot on my mind. I needed to cut Troy off and I wanted to be happy like Cyn. She did invite me to church but I don't think I could do that. If God loved me why was I dealing with crappy men and why did I have to go through all I went through. At this point in my life, I didn't want anything to do with God or the church. I know I needed better I just didn't know where to start.

■■■

   I was awakened to the ringtone to my text messages. I open my eyes and then I tried to close them back because this was my day off and I planned on sleeping in. I grabbed my phone to check my messages and I had two unread messages one from Cyn and one from Troy. I decided to read Cyn's message,

8:30a Cyn: When you love yourself you won't mistreat yourself, so why would you let someone else mistreat you in the name of love

   For the past couple of weeks Cyn's been sending me inspirational messages each morning and I must say they have been helpful. I'm still amazed at how much she has changed. I want to get there but I don't know how and I can't do God. I tried to cut Troy off a few weeks ago but he hit me up and I let him back in but he was no different. I scroll over to his message.

8:17am Troy: You cooking Breakfast?

"*Really, Troy*?" I thought to myself.

Lately our conversations have been real short and he only wants to come over to either eat or have sex. I was feeling used big time. It's like he wants all the benefits of having a girlfriend but he doesn't want me to be his girl. I know I should be pulling away but I realized leaving Troy completely alone would be the hardest thing for me to do.

I hit reply to Troy's message.

8:45a Me: No! I have to drop B.J off at school

I put my phone back on the night stand. I went and took a shower, threw on some clothes. B.J got dressed and I took him to school. After dropping B.J off. I decided to call Troy, because this thing between us was really bothering me. I dialed his number.

"Hello." He said into the phone.

"What's up Troy?"

"Nothing, what's up?"

"Like what's the deal, I can't help but feel like you've been using me lately."

"Man, ain't nobody using you."

"Well, you only call when you want me to cook or when you want to have sex."

"When else am I supposed to call, remember you said you wanted to be friends with benefits."

"When did I say that Troy, you know I've been telling you I want to be with you, you know I love you."

"You don't love me Joy."

"Yes, I do why do you think I keep dealing with you."

"What have I done for you that make you love me."

His question stunned me because I didn't really have an answer. We didn't go out, we didn't do anything romantic and the only time we connected was during sex and outside of sex, we had to force a connection. I had no answer to give him. So, I just snapped at him.

"You know what Troy, whatever, just leave me alone, lose my number, stop texting me and let's just be done for real. I won't call you, let's just end it now!"

"Yo, where is this coming from?" He questioned me.

"Troy really, we don't have to do this, let's be done just go about your business."

"Oh wow, O.K. cool."

I hung up on him and I cried like a child who lost their favorite toy. After running into Cyn and being at the luncheon maybe this was what was supposed to happen.

I needed a man who would love me and I don't know if Troy loved me or not. It was almost 2014 and I wanted a fresh start, I want better and Troy needed to get left behind.

Chapter 26

"When they know, you'll settle for less. They'll give you less"

9:43p Me: Are you on your way home?
9:56p Troy: yea, soon.

 I tried to cut Troy off. I really did. I did good for about three months. I ignored his calls and text and I tried to move forward. I even got back on Tagged and I met a new man who held my interest. His name was Mario and he was very nice, almost too nice. We hung out a few times but it didn't go much further because Troy decided to send me a message pouring his heart out.

 This was something he had never done and I felt like maybe Troy was growing and maybe he realized just how much I meant to him. He asked if I could give him another chance to make things right and he said he was ready for a relationship. I couldn't pass on that, I always wanted to be with Troy and now that he was ready, I couldn't say no. I let Mario go and I gave him another chance.

 We entered an official relationship in May and a week after we began our relationship Troy moved in with me and B.J. I was happy to have Troy live with me, and we became an instant family. We've been together for about four months now and as happy as I was that he finally wanted to be with me our relationship didn't go like I expected.

When Troy initially moved in, he asked if I could give him a break on paying any bills for the first couple of months because he had so many other responsibilities that he needed to catch up on. He had a car note, he had to pay for his daughter's daycare and whatever else she needed and he was paying for some other bills he was in debt to. I wanted him to get on his feet and I didn't feel the need to pressure him about paying rent. I took care of everything and even though he didn't have to pay a thing he still didn't have any money. I would have to loan him money on occasions to help him make it to his next paycheck. I didn't mind helping him because that's what you do when you're in a relationship, you help one another out and in due time he would start helping me out.

A month after we got together I found out Troy was cheating on me. I found out by going through his phone. I was pissed off because I knew something was off but he reassured me that he was being faithful. After our big blow out, he confessed that he was just getting them out of his system and now he was truly ready to be faithful and even though I didn't believe him, I proceeded with the relationship. I was extremely insecure.

When I saw how he talked and texted the other women, it took a toll on my self-esteem because he never talked to me in that manner and I so desperately wished he did. I couldn't trust Troy even when I wanted to something inside of me wouldn't allow me to and that put a few strains on our relationship.

A side from my insecurities, I tried my best to keep him satisfied by doing all the necessary duties a woman should do for her man but he didn't seem to connect with me emotionally like I thought he would and as of

lately I've been feeling like that old *702 songs "I don't really want to stay, I don't want to go"* I just wish Troy would get it together. Somedays he was just so cold and he wouldn't even kiss or hug me when he left or when he came home. The affection was missing, unless we were having sex, then he was connected but I wanted to have that connection outside of sex.

Troy didn't know how to prioritize his time and I was always at the bottom of that list. If he wasn't working, he would hang out with his friends and they got more of his time then I did. These past four months I could count on one hand how many times we've hung out but him and his boys, I could use both of my hands and my feet to count how often he sees them. It was becoming a headache and I found myself begging him for his time.

Every time I thought about leaving. Troy would ask me for my patience, he said this relationship thing was new to him and he has to get used to it. He said he wasn't trying to hurt me, he just has to remember he needs to consider someone else. I gave him my patience because I believed he could be the man I needed and I believed my patience could change him.

It was a little after 11pm and it has been about two hours since Troy's last text and he has yet to walk through the front door. He said he was playing cards with the boys but now I was getting a little suspicious. I decided to send him another text.

11:38p Me: Where are you?
11:49p Troy: On my way home
11:50p Me: You said that 2 hrs. ago
11:51p Troy: we played another game, leaving now
11:52p Me: Yea, ok Troy, a 2-hr. game

He didn't respond to my last text message so I called him. It went straight to voicemail. I called again and it went straight to voicemail. I had to take a few deep breaths, because I was getting upset. I hope he wasn't with some girl. I called again and he finally answered, before he could say hello, I went off.

"Why is your phone going to voicemail?" I shouted into the phone.

"I was making a call! Dang! I'm on my way, you got something sexy on?" He replied.

"Nope!" I said giving him attitude.

"Man, go put something sex on, Ima about to pull up."

He hung up the phone on me.

Even though I was upset with Troy, he did come home every night and I was always told that counts for something. He didn't treat me half as bad as Brian did, so I don't know why I was tripping, he was a decent guy and all I needed to do was be patient with him and eventually he'll come around.

I decided to get a little sexy for Troy, even though my body looked horrible he was the only guy to make me feel comfortable in my nakedness. I put on a leopard matching bra and panty set. I applied my *Japanese Cherry Blossom* lotion from *Bath and Body Works.* I climbed into the bed and waited for him to come in.

Twenty minutes later, Troy stumbled through the door. He came in, undressed and slid into bed with me. He didn't say a word to me. He just started kissing me on my neck and he started feeling on my booty.

We made love, we kissed and he took me to another level of ecstasy. I loved it and I loved him. We connected deeper than we ever have before. He finally released himself and he climbed off me and turned over and went to sleep. I laid there wanting to cuddle, wanting to be held but there he was again being cold after we just shared something so magical. I turned my back towards him.

"Goodnight Troy." I said as tears rolled down my cheeks.

I woke up to the sound of Troy's voice. I overheard him on the phone talking to someone, it sounded like he was agreeing to some plans for tonight. While listening to him, I became a little upset because he promised me we would spend time together tonight but he was making plans with someone else. I turned over towards him as he was ending the call.

"So, you got plans tonight?" I inquired.

"Dang, you nosey," he replied.

"Well, I mean you were talking loud."

"The boys want to get together tonight. Rob's girl just had the baby, they want to go out for drinks."

"Why couldn't ya'll celebrate last night! Didn't ya'll know about the baby?" I said getting a little irritated.

"Last night Rob was at the hospital, tonight he said he wants to get together."

"I thought you said we was hanging out today, you just saw them yesterday."

"We can do something tomorrow."

"Really, Troy, it ain't never about me!" I snapped.

"Chill out Joy, we'll do something tomorrow, I just want to celebrate with Rob, tomorrow will be your day and he leaned over and tried to kiss me.

I moved my head and cut my eyes at him.

"Oh, you mad?" He said laughing as he got up from the bed. "Yo, you have forty dollars I can borrow. Ima go get my haircut and the rest will be for tonight."

"Are you going to give it back when you get paid because it's my phone bill money."

"Yea, I got you."

"You have to get it out my purse."

"Thanks." He said as he grabbed his phone and he walked into the bathroom.

I laid in the bed upset, Troy was leaving and B.J was spending the weekend at Shantel's house and I was going to be spending another night alone. I decided I would lay around in bed all day and stuff my face with ice cream, chips and chocolate. Lately, food has been my comfort every time Troy left me alone. I didn't even know Troy had left until I went into the kitchen to grab a bowl of cereal and some snacks.

"He didn't even bother to tell me bye." I thought to myself, he knew I hated when he did that. I climbed back in bed, with my cereal in hand and turned the TV on and it watched me as I grabbed my cellphone and browsed *Facebook* for a while. My phone buzzed with an incoming text.

10:08a Cyn: Know your worth, when they know you'll settle for less, they'll give you less

Cyn always sent the right messages at what always felt like the right time. I wanted more from Troy and I often wondered was I settling. I remember the Women's Luncheon and they said we teach people how to treat us and maybe I taught Troy that giving me less was ok. I want more from him but I just don't know how to get it.

Chapter 27

"When a person shows you who they are, Believe them"

"Girl, I think I'm going to get this shirt, it goes with that pink pencil skirt I got." I said holding the shirt up so Bridgette and Shantel could look at it.

"Yea, I like that one." Bridgette said.

"Oh yea, that's cute." Shantel replied.

   We were about two weeks away from my birthday trip to D.C and we were out at the mall shopping for a few more outfits.

"I still need a few more accessories." I told the girls.

"*Charlotte Russe* got some cute ones." Shantel said.

"Yes, let's go in there, I need me some black heels." Bridgette added.

We walk into *Charlotte Russe* and I go straight to the accessories and Shantel followed me and Bridgette went over to the shoes.

"I'm so ready to get away." Shantel said.

"Girl! Tell me about it, I'm ready to turn up." I
replied.

"You and me both, I tired of the drama, a getaway it
so needed." Shantel said.

Shantel's been doing o.k. She is still with Desmond.
It's been crazy for her this past year because he had
another baby on her. That situation hurt her to the
core but she let me know that she intends to work it
out with him but I can tell she's getting tired of the
drama and his cheating is draining her, she's not the
same. I grabbed a necklace and two pair of earrings
and we walk over to the shoes to check on Bridgette.

"Oh, Ok girl, those shoes are hot." Shantel said to
Bridgette.

"Ya'll like them?" Bridgette asked.

"Yes!" Shantel and I said in Unison.

"Ya'll sure?" Bridgette asked.

"Yes!" we said again in Unison.

"Girl, go ahead and get the shoes, so we can go." I
said to Bridgette.

Bridgette was my girl and I've grown to love her
just as I love Shantel. She wanted the best for me and
she was always encouraging me.

She was a great mother and she didn't take any mess from men, she didn't stay around for bull crap and I could learn a lot from her.

She was recently proposed to by her man Quan. I tried to be happy for her but jealousy set in as I wished I was in her shoes. I wanted Troy to love me like Quan loved her. We paid for our things and we decided to grab lunch at the food court. I settled on a small fry and a soda from *McDonald's* and made my way back to the table where the girls were sitting.

"So, Joy, what is Troy planning for your birthday?" Bridgette asked.

"He talked about doing dinner and a movie tonight but I don't know." I said sipping my soda, the expression on my face showed I was a little sad.

"Why are you looking like that?" Shantel asked.

"I guess I'm just over it ya'll. I'm over trying to get Troy to spend time with me. It's getting old." I said.

"I'm sure he'll do something for your birthday, I doubt he'll miss it." Shantel said.

"I hope so." I replied.

"You my girl Joy, but you can do so much better than Troy, he's shown you time and time again that he just doesn't care about your feelings." Bridgette said taking a bite of her food.

"Girl, just give him some time, he's a decent dude."
Shantel said.

Bridgette rolled her eyes at what Shantel just said.

"He doesn't need any more time; his time is up."
Bridgette said.

"I hear what you are saying Bridgette, but like Shan
said he is a good dude and I do believe he can change
if I just be patient with him." I said.

"Girl, if he wanted to change, he would have done it
by now. I tell you all the time he is doing what you
allow and he's going to keep doing it when you make
excuses for his behavior. When someone shows you
who they are, believe them."

"I say give it some time, you don't want to lose a
good man because you didn't give him time to grow."
Shantel said.

Bridgette turned her nose up at Shantel.

"Ya'll been together all this time, can you say you're
really happy, I say cut him loose so you can really be
happy." Bridgette said.

I didn't really want to hear what Bridgette was
saying but she was right, Troy hasn't made me happy
and maybe I was better off without him. As much as I
loved Shantel. I was beginning to think her advice
wasn't going to be of any help.

She spent all this time with Desmond being patient and he has yet to change. I had a lot to think about but if Troy didn't do anything for my birthday, he was getting cut off for good. We finished eating and I made my way home.

I grabbed my bags out of the car and went inside the apartment. Before jumping into the shower, I sent Troy a quick text just to confirm our plans for tonight.

6:45p Me: Hey Babe, we still doing something 2nite
6:47p Troy: yeah
6:48p Me: What time will you be home
6:50p Troy: I get off at 7:30, so I'll be home at about 8
6:51p Me: Ok, see you later
6:52p Troy: Yeah

I jumped in the shower and I was so happy about going out with Troy. The last time we went out was to Red Lobster for his birthday back in August. Tonight, was what I needed. I turned the water off and grabbed my towel and applied lotion all over my body. I put on my underclothes and left off my clothes so I could do my hair and make-up. I was in the middle of flat-ironing my hair when I heard Troy come into the house. He came into the bathroom where I was.

"What you are doing?" He asked.

"Seriously, Troy? I'm getting ready. I'm almost done, so you can get in here and shower."

"Naw, I'm not about to get in the shower yet." Troy said.

"Well, what time you trying to leave then? I asked.

"I know you wanted to go out but I don't have no money, so I grabbed us a *RedBox* and some food from *KFC*."

If looks could kill, Troy would be dead on the spot. I was beyond mad. I could feel my heart beating faster.

"So, why did you tell me we were going out to a dinner and a movie?" I snapped.

"I never told you that, you assumed."

"You never clarified either." I yelled at him.

"You never asked." He shot back.

"So, you really think that's good enough for my birthday, did you even get me a gift." I said as I brushed passed him and walked into the kitchen. He followed behind me. I take notice of the *RedBox* and the *KFC* boxes resting on the table and my blood was boiling.

"I can't believe you actually bought a freaking *RedBox* and some chicken for my birthday!" I yelled.

"At least I'm here, you know I'm broke but I did what I could."

"You don't care nothing about me."

"Yo, I do care. If I didn't care I wouldn't be here. I promise I'll make it up to you." He said trying to hug me.

I pushed him off.

"You need to treat me better, you spend your money on what you want, I'm your girl and I don't get a thing! Being your girlfriend hasn't brought me any perks."

"I'm sorry, you know I'm still trying to get adjusted to this whole relationship thing."

"But you were the one that said you were ready." I snapped.

"Yea I did but when you've been single for years, it takes some getting you to."

"It's been almost six months, you should be used to it by now, sometimes I don't even know why you're here."

"I'm here because I care about you."

I didn't say another world, I walked into the living room and Troy followed behind. He grabbed my arm. I turned around to face him.

"Joy, I'm so sorry yo. My money tight you know that but I promise I will start treating you better, let me just show you."

He pulled me close and kissed me. I got a little teary eyed.

"Troy, you say that all the time. Are you really going to do better?" I asked as the tears landed on my cheeks.

He kissed me again. "I promise Joy, don't give up on us, I'll show you, sit down so we can eat."

We sat down at the table and ate our dinner. I was still upset but like Shantel said he was a decent guy and even though he didn't do what I wanted. He did something and I could at least be grateful for that. So, I decided to appreciate his effort instead of being mad about it. He was trying, so why not let him. He made time for me tonight and that was all I really wanted and all of Bridgette's advice about letting him go went out the window.

After dinner, we got comfortable on the couch and he popped the movie into the DVD player. He slid closer to me and he started kissing on my neck. I wanted to stop him but I was weak when it came to Troy.

"Can we make-up?" he whispered in my ear. I didn't give him a response. He pulled my breast out of my bra and he started playing with them. He laid me on my back and he performed oral sex on me and he did some new tricks I had never seen.
 I was all his at that point. He went into the bedroom to grab a condom and he left me on the couch wanting more. He came back and we made sweet love and he lasted longer than he normally does which made for an even better time. It was so good to us, we ended up falling asleep on the floor.

When I woke up to go to the bathroom. I noticed I was laying in the living room alone.

"I know he didn't get up and go in the bedroom and leave me on this floor."

 I pulled myself up off the floor and I walked down the hallway towards the bedroom. I turned on the light and Troy wasn't in the room and he wasn't in the bathroom either.
 I grabbed my cellphone and called Troy. He didn't answer. He sent me a text instead.

10:47p Troy: What's up
10:48p Me: Where are you and answer the phone I just called you.

My phone started ringing and Troy's named flashed across the screen.

"Hello, where are you?" I said into the phone.

"I'll be right back, I ran over to Chris house for a sec. I'll be back in a few." Troy said.

I could feel myself getting upset again, dang I couldn't even get a night to myself. He was always with his boys.

"Dang, I thought we was going to spend the night together." I said into the phone a little irritated.

"We did. We had dinner, we watched a movie and you fell asleep, so I ran out really quick."

"I didn't want just a few hours, I wanted the whole night with you, can I get that?" I snapped into the phone.

"I'll be back yo. I'll be back home in about twenty minutes. I just came to holla at him about something."

"You couldn't call him and tell him?" I asked.

"He wanted to show me something. Chill out!"

"Whatever, Troy it's the same crap, like you just promised you would change!"

"Yea, I know that but I can't change in a day but I'm working on it. I'll be home in a few."

"You just keep showing me you don't care, you keep showing me who you really are, and I need to just believe it and be done with you!" I yelled into the phone before hanging up on him.

Troy didn't even bother to call me back and maybe it was time for me to take heed to Bridgette's advice and walk away. Troy just didn't care.

Chapter 28

"Something Doesn't feel Right"

I sat at work watching the clock go by. There was fifteen minutes left in my shift and I was ready to go. It's been a few days since my birthday incident and I haven't cut Troy off, he's says he will change and he just needs my patience. I agreed to be patient for a little while longer if I see he is changing. I watched the clock as it seemed to move even slower. I had five more minutes left and I couldn't wait to clock out. Troy promised he would take me out tonight to make-up for my birthday incident and because I was leaving tomorrow to go to D.C with the girls. I just hope he does what he promised.

It was finally time for me to clock-out and I rushed out of the door and hopped in the car and I went to go get B.J from his aftercare program. I dropped him off with Ms. Ann who agreed to keep him for the weekend. I was so happy she said yes because I had no one else to keep him. Initially Brian was doing O.K., he would come get B.J every other weekend but then he fell of the wagon, he stopped asking for B.J and he stopped calling him, last, I heard from one of his other baby mother's is that he was in Jail because he assaulted some woman he use to deal with. I still hate him for how he left me and B.J so if he suffers he deserve every bit of it.

I kissed B.J and thanked Ms. Ann and hopped in the car and spun down the road so I could get ready for tonight. After what happened last time I didn't get dressed until Troy came home and he confirmed that we were going out. I put on the outfit I was going to wear last weekend. It was a dark blue long sleeve body con dress and I was just glad the weather cooperated so I could wear it. I pulled out my girdle so it would hide some of the fat I gained over the past months. It was weird how I could feel comfortable being naked in front of Troy but I still hated every inch of my body. I despised it and I never really felt comfortable in my own skin but it was Brian that made me feel the worse.

He made sure he engrained fat and ugly in my head and those definitions of my beauty stuck with me after all those years and even though Troy was around he couldn't heal those wounds. I pulled my hair back into a low ponytail. I applied a little make-up and I went into the living room and waited for Troy to finish up. Troy was finally ready and we hopped in the car and drove over to *Outback*.

We walked in and I was so glad it wasn't packed. The hostess walked us to our booth and we slid into the booth. I couldn't help but notice this light skin girl staring at me with her face screwed up. I tried to pay it no mind and went ahead and ordered my drink but when I looked up, she was staring again.

"Troy, do you see that girl over there she keeps staring at me, do you know her."

"Naw, I don't know what's her problem."

"You sure you don't know her, she's definitely staring over here."

"Naw, I don't know that girl." He insisted.

"Well she better get it together before I have to handle her."

"Joy, be cool. Let's just order our food."

We ordered our food and that light skin girl was really on something tonight, she would not stop looking at us and I was getting pissed off every time I noticed her looking my way. Our food arrived and I tried to eat my food but I couldn't because light skin got up and came over to our table. My face had attitude written all over it.

"Hey, Troy." She said.

I gave Troy a look of death.

"Oh, what's up." He replied.

"How have you been." She said.

"Um, who are you? I interjected. She ignored me and kept right on talking to Troy.

"How have you been?" She asked him again.

"I'm good, how about you?" he replied.

My blood was boiling, not only was I pissed that she came over to my table interrupting my dinner but that Troy was entertaining her.

"I'm doing well, nice seeing you again." She said.

"Good, seeing you too." Troy said.

"I'm Joy, I'm Troy's girlfriend." I said with an attitude.

Troy had a nervous look on his face and everything about him not knowing her was a complete lie. I was ready to go off.

"Oh, hi." She said dry and dismissive. Then she focused her eyes back on Troy. "See you around." She said as she walked off.

"See you around, Troy, really, who the hell is she, I thought you didn't know her?" I snapped.

"I don't know her like that, Rob girl had a birthday dinner and she was there. I really don't know her."

"Yea. Whatever Troy, stop lying. It's more to it, the way she was staring, are you messing around with her."

"I can't tell nobody what to do with their eyes, and I don't know her like that."

"I can't tell, she seems to really like you."

"I met her at the party and that's it. I can't help who likes me, you need to chill out, you act like I told her to come over here."

"You let her come over and disrespect me and you didn't even bother introducing me."

"You didn't give me time Joy, I'm not about to do this. I'm out trying to celebrate your birthday and you tripping about some chick I don't even know."

"It just doesn't feel right, you ain't telling me everything. She didn't pay me any mind and when I tried to introduce myself she didn't even care. I know something doesn't feel right."

"Man, come on if I was messing with her, she would've acted worse than that."

"Maybe, maybe not, but the way she was just staring makes me think something happened with ya'll."

"I can't help who wants me." He said with a smile.

"Oh whatever." I chuckled.

Troy kept reassuring me that nothing happened between him and light skin. I wanted to believe him but something just didn't feel right. My mind went into overload. I was torn in two. Part of me felt like it was my insecurities that was causing me to overreact and that maybe Troy was right, she liked him and she was mad that he was with me.

The other part of me felt like Troy was lying about the whole thing. Troy has been known to lie before and Bridgette did say when a person shows you who they are believe them. Troy has shown me he is a liar. I mean he lied tonight, he claimed he didn't know her when he did, so what makes me think he's not lying about messing with her. I was all over the place and I didn't know what to think or do.

We made our way home and I couldn't stop thinking about Light Skin from the restaurant and everything that just played out. I wanted to believe Troy but I just didn't know. We walked in the house and we both got undressed and I couldn't help but ask Troy about Light Skin again.

"So, you ain't messing with her?" I asked taking off my underwear and putting on my night gown.

"Yo, I told you no, I don't know her like that." He said as he climbed into the bed.

"Something just ain't sitting right with me." I said climbing into bed next to him.

"We going to keep talking about that or we going to enjoy our night." He said leaning over to kiss me on my neck.

"I want to enjoy the night but I can't help but think about what happened and how you lied."

"Man, what I lie about?" he snapped.

"You said you didn't know her but you did."

"Yo, you really trying to talk about this. I told you I don't know her only seen her at a party." He yelled. "Dang, why are you tripping."

"So, why lie? why wouldn't you just say you met her at the party, oh it's probably because you didn't think she would've came over to talk to us, because I'm sure if she never got up you would still be saying you don't know her."

"Man, you really about to do this?" He said sitting up in the bed.

"Yea, cause you lying about something."

"Man, what do I have to do to show you that I ain't messing with her or nobody?" He snapped.

"Let me see your phone, show me your text messages." I snapped back.

"Naw, what my phone got to do with this?"

"If you ain't cheating let me see your phone, why won't you show me."

"Because you don't pay my bill, so you don't need to look at my phone." He yelled back.

"Oh really, but I pay for everything else." I said mushing him in the head.

"Yo, man!" He said as he got up from the bed. "Why you hit me!"

"You such a liar, if you weren't cheating, just show me your phone and it would be all good!" I yelled.

"Because I don't have to, it's my phone, I ain't got to show you, take my word. I ain't doing nothing!" He yelled. "I ain't about to do this with you tonight, man I'm out, I'll be at Chris'."

   Even though I was angry and upset that he wouldn't show me his phone. I wanted him home with me and I would do anything to keep him home. So, I calmed myself down so that he would get back in the bed. I apologized to him and told him I take his word even though I really didn't. I performed oral sex on him so that he would believe I believed him. We had sex and he fell asleep. I couldn't go to sleep, I had to see what was inside his phone.

Troy was out, snoring and all. I tipped toed over to his side of the bed and his phone was on the floor beside the bed. I was so nervous; my heart was beating fast. I finally grab the phone and I ran into the living room. He had a passcode on his phone. I tried every combination I could think of and nothing worked and I got pissed off all over again. I tipped toed back into the room and put his phone back on the floor. I'll let it go tonight but something didn't feel right about Light Skin. The best proof would be time and I know that in due time I would know the truth and I hoped that it would be Troy's truth.

Chapter 29

"Love Grows...Love Doesn't Destroy"

I hear my alarm ringing in my ear. I turned over and turned it off. It was a little after 8 am. I was tired after being up late trying to break into Troy's phone. I hopped in the shower and got dressed. In the middle of doing my hair, I hear my phone ringing from the other room. I run into the other room to grab my phone and it was Shantel.

"Hello, I said excitedly.

"Happy Birthday Sis, Turn up boo! Turn up boo!" She yelled into the phone. "You Ready?"

"Thank you, yea just doing my hair really quick. You on the way?"

"Yeah, in about ten minutes. You talk to Bridgette?" She asked.

"Naw, not this morning but I texted her last night to tell her to meet me at my house at about 9am." I replied.

"Ok, see you in a few."

"Alright, bye."

Before I could put the phone down. I noticed two text messages. One was from Cyn and the other was from Troy. I scrolled over to Cyn's message first.

8:38a Cyn: Love GROWS...Love Doesn't DESTROY

Cyn was very encouraging her messages always came on time. I scrolled over to Troy's message.

8:36a   Troy: GM have a great day

I decided to reply back to Troy's message.

8:49a Me: I will because it's my Birthday!! ☺
8:52a Troy: Oh, my bad, Happy Birthday!
8:53a Me: Really, Troy?

   I waited for a reply and he never sent one; *"Typical Troy."* I thought to myself. I was little pissed. I put the phone down and continued doing my hair.
   The girls finally arrived and we packed our bags in Shantel's truck. 95 North here we come. About two and a half hours into our drive. I could feel my phone vibrating on my legs. It was Troy.

12:19p   Troy: Wyd?
12:20p   Me: Oh, now you reply
12:22p   Troy: Don't start, wyd
12:24p   Me: On the road

12:27p   Troy: Who driving?

12:28p   Me: Shan

12:32p   Troy: oh ok

12:35p   Me: Troy we should come up here one weekend, just me and you.

12:29p   Troy: I'll see

12:30p   Me: What you mean you'll see

12:36p   Troy: Don't know if I'll have extra money

12:38p   Me: I'll pay for the room

12:44p   Troy: I'll still let you know, did you leave the money

12:46p   Me: Yes, I left it in my top drawer, wyd

1:12 p   Troy: working, have fun, I'll text you later

1:14p   Me: ok be good, don't have nobody in my house lol

1:18p   Troy: Chill out

1:20p   Me: Ok, ttyl

Sometimes I wish Troy wouldn't even bother texting me. Even though he said he was changing it seems like I have to pull a conversation out of him which I'm tired of doing. I put my phone down and laid my head back and took a nap for the rest of the way.

We finally arrived at our hotel. We got settled in and I was so ready for the weekend and glad to be away. I texted Troy to let him know that we made it. His reply was short and dry, Troy knew how to work my nerves. I tried to pay it no mind, so I could enjoy my weekend but I couldn't let it go. I go into the bathroom and I decide to call him instead. The first time I called he didn't answer. The second call he sent me straight to voicemail. My blood was boiling. I was furious. I called him again and he finally answered.

"Yo, what's up?" He said into the phone.

"I texted you and called you." I snapped into the phone.

"Yo, I replied!"

"yea, but it seems like you don't want to be bothered."

"You said you made it, I said ok, what did you want me to say."

"Anything, have fun, enjoy your birthday, I miss you, I love you, something that shows you care."

"Joy, you all the way in D.C. Why are you tripping? Go have fun with your girls. I'll text you later."

"You know what! Whatever Troy!" I hung up on him.

Tears rolled down my cheek and I was tired of Troy, and trying to make him love me back. He said he was ready for this, he said he wanted a relationship but ever since we've got together it seems like he just doesn't want me like he claims he does. I'm just ready for him to change.

"Come on Joy! Let's take some Shots!" Bridgette yell through the bathroom door.

"I'm coming!" I yelled through the door. I got myself together and came out of the bathroom.

I thought I got myself together but I guess I couldn't hide my pain. Bridgette could see it all in my face.

"What's wrong now?" Bridgette asked.

"I'm just tired of Troy."

"I told you to leave him alone, he's a bum and don't let him ruin your birthday weekend. Matter of fact you're ignoring him all weekend." Bridgette said. "Here, take this shot and let's turn up.

We took a couple more shots. Shantel turned the music up and we turned up. Bridgette was right. This was my weekend of fun and I wasn't going to let Troy ruin it for me. We took turns showering. We got dressed. Bridgette did my hair and my make-up. We looked good and we were ready for some Fun. It was my freaking Birthday. It was time to turn up.

The weekend flew by and D.C showed me a great time. It was just what I needed. Troy did hit me up and while I ignored him the first night of our trip. I couldn't ignore him the second night, I had to reply because I was tired of having these mixed emotions and I was hoping him and I could figure out things.

It was bittersweet leaving D.C. I had a blast and didn't want to go back to my reality but I did miss Troy and B.J and I was ready to get back to them. We made it back to Columbia in no time. I swear it seems like Bridgette was doing over a hundred on the highway. Bridgette pulled up to my apartments and I was so happy to see Troy's car.
Shantel's Brother Micah was going to drop B.J off after they leave the basketball court. Which gave me some alone time with Troy. The girls and I exchanged hugs and kisses and we parted ways.

I dragged myself up the stairs with my suitcase in hand up to my apartment. I slid my key into the lock and opened the door and the first thing that hit me was the sound of Beyoncé's "Dance for You". "What is he doing?" I thought to myself. I left my suitcase at the door and made my way down the hall to the bedroom. I grabbed the handle and opened the door.

"Hey ba— "

I couldn't even finish my sentence; my man Troy was laid across my bed naked and there was a light skinned woman between his legs giving him oral sex. They looked at me dead in my face and then I noticed it was Light Skin from the restaurant. I lost it and I snapped. All I saw was red and I jumped for her. I went crazy and I blacked out.

When I came to, Troy was holding me back and Light Skin ran out of my room and I'm assuming out of my apartment. I started fighting Troy. I gave him a combination of punches. I was enraged. I kept punching him and then he grabbed me and shook me and then pushed me on the bed.

"Joy, stop let me explain."

"Explain, What!" I yelled as I got off the bed and went straight to the closet for his things. He tried to block me and I started punching him again. He grabbed my arms and tried to make me stop.

"Get out of my house!" I yelled. "Get out of my house!" Tears and snot was running down my face. "Get the hell out, get all of your mess and get the hell out! Leave! Leave!"

"Joy, I messed up, I'm sorry." He said trying to hug me.

I pushed him off. "LEAVE, LEAVE, LEAVE!! I yelled. "Do you need help leaving!" I went back to the closet and grabbed several and ran into the living room he followed behind and I threw his shirts outside in front of my apartment.

"Really, Joy. You throwing me out?"

I stood there with the door opened.

"LEAVE!" I yelled. "Do I need to throw more of your stuff out! Leave Troy!"

He tried to hug me again.

"Don't freaking touch me, leave me alone Troy! Get out of my house! Bye! Bye! Bye!" I yelled to the top of my lungs.

"Really, Joy?"

"The door is open, get the out of my house!"

He didn't say another word, he went back in the room and I followed behind him. He slipped on some clothes and I grabbed some of his other clothes and as he walked out the door, I threw some more of his clothes outside of my apartment. I did this a couple more times until all his things were laying outside my apartment.

I closed the door. I fell to the floor. My tears could fill up a bathtub. I was humiliated, embarrassed, mad, sad, my heart was breaking once again. I couldn't breathe. My heart-ached. Now it all makes sense and now I know that Light Skin was his side piece and he was cheating on me the whole time.

"WHY!" I screamed out.

"WHY!"

I hear my phone ringing from inside of my purse. I grabbed my phone out of my purse and it was Troy. I ignored his first four calls. The fifth call I answered.

"What!" I yelled into the phone.

"Joy, I'm sorry, yo."

"No, you're not you had a hoe in my house."

"Forgive me, I got caught up. I didn't mean to hurt you. I want us to work. I love you in case you don't know."

"If you love me why did you have that hoe in my house. After everything Brian put me through, you turn around and do the same thing."

"Yo, I ain't him and I do love you."

"You ain't no better."

"Joy, give me another chance, I will do right. You the one I want to be with. Can I come back tonight?"

"I don't know, you really hurt me. I don't know."

"Give me a chance, I won't hurt you again."

"I don't know, you've said that too many times. Just leave me alone!" I hung up the phone on him.

He called back several times but I ignored his calls. I picked myself up off the floor and I laid myself across the couch. I was disgusted, Troy had another girl in my bed, in my apartment. I wallowed in my own tears and all I could think about was Cyn's Message that said, "Love Grows, Love Doesn't Destroy" and I realized Troy's love never grew me, he brought nothing to my life all it did was destroy me.

Chapter 30

"Who's going to Love me?"

"Yea, I just texted you my address, did you get it?" I said.

"Yea, I got it. I'll be over in a few." Johnathan said into the phone.

After I caught Troy in my house, I was so crushed. I couldn't believe he would do that to me. He hurt me in the worst way. I had to call out of work three days straight because I didn't feel like doing anything or dealing with anyone. Troy tried to comeback, he called me for several days after I kicked him out and I was doing good. I ignored him and I was proud of myself because I desperately wanted to answer the phone.

I was being strong until he showed up at my door one night and he was looking so cute and as much as I tried to fight against it, I became weak in his presence. I let him in and we had sex. We tried to do the relationship thing again but it just didn't work. We tried for about a month and a half and he still wouldn't do right. I was still begging for him to show me some affection and he just wouldn't.

I was just getting fed up but what broke the camel's back was when I contracted a STD from him the fourth time I let him have sex with me without a condom. If he was being faithful, I would have never got the STD. When I confronted him, he had the nerve to say I was the one that probably gave it to him and he had the nerve to say that he was done with me. I was devastated. I let him back in my life after what he did and then he burns me literally and then he leaves me and blames me for the STD. I cried for days after he left but Shantel encouraged me to move on and find someone else to help me get over Troy.

I changed my number and I started talking to Eric. He was very cool down to earth kind of guy. He was someone I could see a future with but he was only around for about three and a half weeks because after I had sex with him. He didn't bother to call again.

Then there was Marcel. He was fine. He was a car salesman and he made good money. He did take me out on dates and we had a good time together but he was too nice and I felt like I could run over him. He called me and text me frequently and I never had to beg him to spend time with me and he wanted to do things with me outside of sex. I wasn't used to that. Marcel really liked me and I couldn't deal with it, he was too soft. Once I slept with him, he wanted to be with me but I couldn't do it. So, I moved on with Julian.

Julian was half black and Puerto Rican and he wasn't the best looking but he was cool. We smoked weed together and we got drunk together. He was trying to be a rapper. He was funny and we had fun together.

We hung out with each other for about month or so after we had sex a couple of times he started pulling away and eventually he stopped answering my calls.

Now I have my boo Johnathan. Johnathan is my light skin cutie. He is tall and he reminds me of Drake the rapper. We have become real cool.

We haven't slept together yet. It's been about two weeks and him and I just clicked and he talks about building a future with me and I can see us doing that. He kept me on my toes and I never knew what I would get with him. Tonight, was the night I planned on sleeping with him. He was cute and I wanted to win him over. He seemed like he like me. I cooked us a nice dinner and afterwards I planned on taking it to the next level.

I cleaned up the house and cooked spaghetti and garlic bread. Pasta was my favorite thing to cook. He knocked on the door. I opened it and he looked so good and he smelled so good. He came in and we sat down and had dinner and the conversation was great. He was so smart and he just drew me in with his intelligence. We took our conversation from the table to the couch as we talked about our future. He said he really liked me and he want to make me his girl.

He leaned over and kissed me and it sent chills down my spine.

I was ready to jump on him right then and there. He kept kissing me and I could feel myself getting turned on.

I stood up from the couch and I grabbed his hand and pulled him up and lead him towards my bedroom. Once inside the bedroom, I sat him on the bed and I performed oral sex on him.

I blew his mind. I gave him a condom out of my drawer and he put it on and I rocked his world. His sex was amazing and I wanted to be with him so bad. He was everything I ever wanted.

Once we were done we laid down in my bed and we just talked. I felt so comfortable with him. He was just so different and I was so happy to even be in his presence and I was so glad that a man like him wanted a girl like me. He decided not to stay the night and I was sad that he had to leave but he made plans for us to see each other tomorrow.

■■

It's been about three weeks since I've been with my boo Johnathan and things were going surprisingly good. He never stayed the night but he did make his way over to see me every evening which I liked. I did everything for him, I cooked for him and I gave him good sex. He was good with B.J and I could see us building a family. Johnathan made me happy. I don't think I would've ever been happy if I hadn't met him. What did I do to be this lucky I thought to myself as I browsed around on *Facebook*, then I noticed under the *People you May Know* section a picture of what look liked Johnathan under the name James Roberts Jr. and it was a photo of him with a girl and three children.

I clicked on the profile but everything was private except for the profile picture. I took a screenshot of the profile and I texted it to Johnathan letting him know someone was using his picture. I never got a reply. I called him but he kept sending me to voicemail. I called him a few more times that day and he never answered.

I thought he was going to be my dream guy but I realized that he was just like every other man I had been with. To put the icing on the cake he didn't even care to give me an explanation. He just cut off the communication and discarded me and pushed me to the side when he realized his cover was blown. I was a wreck because I just knew he was the one. I just knew he would be my forever. We just clicked and I felt so happy with him. But he was another liar and cheater. I was so tired of getting used and pushed to the side by men. I was tired of just being good enough for sex but no one pursued anything more. I was tired of men. I started to hate men at this point because all they did was take, no one wanted to give me anything. All I ever wanted was to be happy. I just wanted someone to love me. I just wanted to be loved. Is there anybody out there who's going to love me? I'm not asking for much am I?

Chapter 31

"Where's My Joy"

It's been about a week since Johnathan just ignored me and left me hanging and I was tired of men. I found myself taking up residence on my couch trying to make sense of my life. I was tired and I wanted to know what did I do to deserve what he did to me. I just want to be loved and I thought he would be the one to do that but he played with my heart like all the guys in my past have done.

Am I not good enough? Maybe I'm not good enough to be loved. No one ever wanted to love me like the love I see in the movies. No one ever made me the center of their world. All I ever wanted was for someone to be happy to have me, to be happy about the way I looked. Happy about loving me.

I got up from the couch and went to the bathroom. While washing my hands,I glanced at my reflection in the mirror and I looked horrible. Maybe it's because I wasn't beautiful like those other girls. I wasn't pretty. My skin was dark, my lips was big and I was fat. I wasn't the ideal beauty and maybe that's why I couldn't get a man to love me. They all cheated on me with other women, women I assume was better looking than me.

I was so ugly. I rubbed my hands across my face several times and then starred at myself again in the mirror.

"You're ugly Joy, that's why they don't want you, that's why they never loved you, you don't have the look, you aren't who they really want, you aren't good enough, look at your black skin, look at your dark black skin. Who would want you and that stomach, you're so fat Joy, all you do is eat, all you do is eat, you're so stupid and dumb and ugly, that's why they don't want you, that's why they don't love you!" I yelled to my reflection and tears just fell down my cheeks.

I walked out of the bathroom and into the kitchen and opened the refrigerator and realized I had no beer. I closed the refrigerator angrily and went to lay back on the couch. I'm so glad B.J spent the weekend with Bridgette because I don't want him seeing me this way.

I am unlovable, my own mother didn't love me enough to fight to live to stay here with me. She left me and then my damn daddy left me and then I had to go move with those people my stupid grandmother and that bastard of a grandfather. Ms. Ann said he died about a month ago, from a heart attack and I didn't shed not one tear, that's what the hell he gets.

Why didn't my family want me? Why didn't they love me enough? What was it about me that they hated so much? I wanted my daddy to want me. Why didn't he come back for me? Why did he abandon me and run off to live his life, was I not good enough? Did he not have love for me, did he not feel one ounce of love for me? Why didn't my grandmother protect me? Why was she so mean and hateful? Why didn't she kiss me or hug me or tell me how special I am? Why did my grandfather touch me like he did, why did he make me give him my body? Why would he want to hurt me that way? I still don't understand why, why he would do that when he could have had sex with my grandmother. Why did he want me? My pain started with my family, they made me feel unloved and unworthy when they abandoned me. They left me in a cold world alone. They deserted me when I wanted to be loved, when I wanted them to want me. They did this, they did this, they did this to me.

"Why didn't my family love me!" I screamed out into the living room.

There were so many times I wanted to end my life because it got too hard, it became too stressful, every man I loved left me and every time I tried, I saw B.J and I just couldn't do it. Why didn't my mother think of me, why didn't she think about the little girl she birthed, why did she leave me alone in this world with no one to love me? Why didn't she stay with me? I needed her to love me. I needed her to stay Alive.

"Where is the person who will love me?" I yelled out into the living room. Tears falling profusely down my face.

I've been hurt, I've been abused by people I loved and I tried to keep them happy. I was willing to do anything to keep them happy so they wouldn't give up on me. I needed their love, I need someone's love. I put up with so much to keep a man in my life because I wanted to feel what real love felt like.

I gave them my body, my money, me and they didn't give me a thing but pain and then they discarded and abandoned me, they left me for other women. Why wasn't I good enough. I hate myself. I wasn't the woman, men wanted for forever. They loved my body and my sex but I wasn't who they wanted to be with. I wasn't good enough.

Who could blame them. I mean who would want a woman who've had sex with countless men, who've aborted four of her own babies and who couldn't stay pregnant. Who wants a woman who use to dance naked for money and who sold her body to men? A woman whose vagina has been infected with a numerous amount of STD's. Who would want me? Nobody would want that, I was damaged and nobody wants a broke down damaged woman, maybe that's why every man I ever loved cheated on me because I am unsuitable for love.

Not to mention the abuse. I was beat lifeless at times. The broken ribs and broken body parts and the abuse to my face. The verbal abuse was the most damaging. Every man I let into my life picked away at my self-esteem, which I didn't have much of to begin with and they made me feel even lower. They destroyed the way I felt about me, I saw myself through their eyes and in their eyes, I wasn't a good thing, I was unlovable.

My life has been nothing but pain and it seems like it won't ever get better. I'm tainted. I'm cursed, from the day I took my first breathe my life has been cursed.

I remember my mother saying she named me Joy because I would bring Joy into their lives and I couldn't even do that. I haven't brought Joy to anyone's life. I don't even know why she named me Joy because the only Joy I've ever had was my name. Where was my Joy? When will I feel happy? When will I see Joy? I waited all my life for a relief to feel the Joy my mother said I would bring and that Joy never came. My name should have been unlovable, failure, stupid, fat, ugly, murderer, unworthy, whore because those are true statements about me but Joy, Joy ain't never came to visit me.

"Where you at joy?" I yelled out.

"Well, joy where are you?" I yelled out again.

"Why haven't you come by to see me!" I scream out. Tears swell up in my eyes and fall on my cheeks one by one. I don't know what to do, I just want to feel worthy. I just want to feel like I'm worth being loved. I just want to be happy. I just want some Joy in my life, because I'm hurting and in so much pain, I'm so broken, I've been beaten down to shreds. I don't like myself.

I hate myself for what I've done and who I am. I blamed God for giving me this life, I hated the cards I've been dealt. God why won't you just take it away. Give me a new life. God why did you leave me and not protect me. God where are you. God do you care?

I hear my text message ringtone go off and I grab my cellphone off the floor and checked my text message. I scroll over and realize it was from Cyn.

8:33p Cyn: You can't afford to give up on you. You will overcome your situation. Just believe it! Your better is out there. Praying for your strength tonight.

I broke down crying. Her messages always came at the right time. I just laid there crying letting every painful memory flow out with each tear that fell on my cheek. Maybe some people just aren't worthy of knowing Joy, maybe some people just aren't good enough to know Joy. Maybe I was that person who wasn't worthy enough, but I wanted to know Joy, I wanted to know what it felt like.

I stayed put on the couch for the rest of the night, weeping. I hated myself and my life.

Chapter 32

"You're not the only one"

"I'm on the way." I said in to my phone. "I should be there in ten minutes."

"Ok, you're still coming, Right?" Cyn asked.

"Yes, I am girl, my GPS took me in the wrong direction. I should be there in a few minutes."

"Ok, see you soon. Thank you for coming.

I was on my way to Cyn's house for a girl's night in. She invited me and Bridgette and a couple of her other friends. It was just what I needed after everything I've been going through. Cyn was a great person and she has always looked out for me and I was grateful to have her in my life.

It hasn't been easy for me and I've been struggling lately within and trying to make sense of the life I've been dealt. After my break down that night Julian hit me up again and I was happy to hear from him. He came over that night and we had sex and we've been sleeping together now for the past two weeks and things have been o.k. Even though I want a relationship with him, he doesn't and I accepted that just so I wouldn't have to be alone.

I finally pulled up to Cyn's house and it was beautiful. It was a modern two-story home. She lives in a subdivision in the nice part of town. She was doing very well. I parked on the curb in between her and her neighbor's house. I grabbed my bag out the back of the car and walked up to the door and rang the doorbell.

"Well, hello glad you finally showed up." Bridgette said sarcastically.

"Oh, whatever." I said as we exchanged hugs.

"Hey ladies! Joy is here!" Bridgette announced to the other ladies. They were all sitting on the couch with glasses of wine talking.

"Hey Joy!" They all said in unison.

"Hey, Joy. Come here let me introduce you to some ladies I call my big sisters. These are the ladies who mentored me and helped me get on the right track." Cyn said.

I walked over to the couch.

"This is Mia." Cyn said as she pointed to a tall brown skin woman. She reminded me of Kimberly Elise.

We exchanged handshakes.

"and this is Arielle she may be little but she is a firecracker." Cyn said laughing.

Arielle stood up to hug me. "I don't do handshakes, we're family now." Arielle said.
"Joy you want something to eat?" Bridgette said as she walked towards the kitchen.

"Naw, I'm good right now." I replied.

"You want some wine?" Cyn asked.

"Yea, I'll take that." I said.

"Bri, can you grab Joy a glass of wine." Cyn asked.

I took a seat on the vacant sofa and Bridgette brought me my glass of wine. She took her seat next to me. Then Cyn stood up.

"Ladies, thank you for coming. I invited you all here for some girl chat. Where we can discuss anything under the sun that will help us with whatever we may be going through. I want to begin by saying a prayer. Can we all stand up." Cyn said.

I was a little hesitant to stand up. I haven't prayed since I was a little girl at church but since everyone else stood up I followed suite. I just hoped we wasn't going to be talking about God all night. Cyn prayed and afterwards the girl chat began. Cyn had each of us write different questions about things going on around us and we put them into a coffee mug and we were going to discuss them one by one. Bridgette pulled the first question out of the mug and read it.

"Alright here it goes ladies. Do you think the best way to get over an old man is to get under a new man?"

"I used to" Bridgette said. "It used to make sense and I lived by it, why sweat one man when you could just move on but then Cyn taught me another way"

I jumped in "I mean why not, there's always somebody else and they can help you get over the other guy."

"But then you take the unresolved baggage and bitterness into the next relationship it's really best to take some alone time after each relationship so you can heal your heart." Cyn said.

"I've never been alone, when one mess up. I move on to the next. I've always had a man in my life." I said.

"How did those relationships turn out?" Cyn asked.

"Not good." I replied laughing.

"I was like that too. I always needed some man in my life. Single, married or whatever I just needed one in my life. I didn't want to be by myself so I settled for any man that showed me some attention. I let them use me and the irony behind it all is even though I was with them because I didn't want to be alone. They made me feel alone anyway, I had to grow to learn that healing is so necessary before moving forward. I had to learn that it's ok to want and need a man but you don't settle for just any man to cure your loneliness." Mia said.

"I don't know if I could be alone, like not dealing with anyone." I said.

"Yea, I thought that too until I finally felt real peace, and realized being alone is better than dealing with bull crap." Mia said.

"Maybe one day I'll get there." I replied.

"Ok, Joy your turn to pick the next question." Cyn said.

I dug my hand into the coffee mug and pulled out a slip of paper and read the question.

"Do you think all men cheat? I said.

Cyn and Mia and Arielle replied "No."

"Really no?" I questioned.

"I used to believe they all did before I met Quan but I don't think they all do." Bridgette said.

"Joy, I thought so too but all men aren't the same and there are some faithful men out here."Cyn said.

"That's just weird that ya'll said no, because every man I know has cheated all the way back to my granddad and my dad and every man I've ever been with cheated." I said.

"Joy, would you believe me if I told you that there are good men out here, who don't cheat." Mia said.

"Yea that's hard to believe, I've always been taught that cheating is just a man being a man." I said.

"I was just like you, every man on this planet was a cheater and you couldn't tell me differently. It wasn't until I healed that I realized that cheating is unhealthy behavior and not all men partake in it. Back in the day our women were taught that cheating was part of a man's make-up and that when a man cheats it should be excused because that's what men do and that's misguided advice that's been passed on to women after women. A man that's constantly cheating is an unhealthy man. I've been married now for about twelve years and my husband hasn't been unfaithful." Mia said.

"Maybe you just didn't find out." I said.

"Oh, no baby girl. I believe in a saying that says What's done in the dark will come out into the light, so I would have known, we all know." Mia replied.

"I just can't believe that, I've never met a man that didn't cheat, this is new to me." I said.

"I think we all use to feel like that, but soon you'll see." Bridgette said.

"Not all men are bad or unfaithful, I'm telling you love doesn't constantly hurt, it's not perfect but it shouldn't constantly hurt."Arielle said.

I could feel myself getting a little emotional just talking about cheating made me think about all the cheating I've put up with and to hear cheating isn't something men do, it made me sad.

"Love for me has always been hard and full of pain. It's hard to believe love could feel any other way." I said. Tears swelled up in my eyes. "I'm sorry ya'll. I didn't mean to cry."

Cyn handed me some tissues. "No that's what tonight is about helping one another overcome situations that's bothering us."Cyn said.

"Over these few years I've just been through a lot. I keep hearing about these "good relationships" I call them fairytales because none of them ever happened to me.

"I once struggled like you baby girl. I grew up in the home with both my parents but they were devout Christians and my dad was a deacon at the church and they were strict any and everything was the devil and we couldn't do a thing. We went to church Sunday through Thursday for some type of service. I was a good kid, did what they asked. Then I went off to college and I was introduced to a whole new world. I was introduced to sex and weed and alcohol and I was partying heavy. The first time I had sex in college, I got pregnant. My parents were mad but I had the baby. A year later I got pregnant by another man, had the baby and you know my parents were furious. I had to drop out of school. Two years later I had another baby by a man I met at the church. My parents wanted to disown me because I was 23 with three children. You would've thought I learned my lesson but I found myself pregnant by another man one year later. At the age of twenty-five my parents forced me to tie my tubes since I was living with them. After that I still slept around with whomever showed me some attention, like I told ya'll before it didn't matter if they were single or married, if they wanted me I let them have me. I let men use and dog me out. I was hurt bad by men I loved. What changed everything for me is when I was diagnosed with HIV and it felt like I got rolled over by a truck. I took it hard and felt like I was worthless. I shut everyone out and tried to fight the battle alone. It was tough and I had no one to turn to but God. I remembered how to pray from being in the church. I started seeking God for answers and just to have someone to cry to and I had to deal with every single emotion. I had to heal every place I was broken. I had to dig deep to heal. I found support groups in my area and I started attending them regularly and they've helped me tremendously. I went to counseling through the doctor I went to. I took control over the disease, I stopped letting it control my life. I decided to live and enjoy the life I still had. I took control of my health and it's over 20 years and I haven't had to take a pill yet. God is so amazing! I started to love myself for who I was and not for the things I've done or that was done to me. God restored everything back to me. I met my now husband at the new church I attend and he accepted me with my children and HIV. He loves me for me and it's because he loves me the way Christ does. So, you're not the only one who has had painful relationships, I have to, but with God all things can change around for you. I take it a day at a time but with God those days are easier to get through when you know you will come out." Mia said.

"Oh wow, you don't even look like you've been through all that." I said.

"We all have a story to tell, when I say you're not alone, you aren't. Many of us have been dealt a hand we didn't really want to play and then some of us put ourselves in the situations, but the one thing I've learned is that if you want better you can have it, it's out here for you." Mia said.

"But how do you get better, where do you start?

"Can I share my story with you Joy?" Arielle asked.

"Yea, you can." I replied.

"It may look like I have it all together too but baby, it's all due to God. You talked about fairytales but my life wasn't a fairytale. I was born to a heroine addicted mother and my father wasn't around. In the early eighties, my mother found a new addiction and she got hooked on Crack. I remember when I was about six or seven my mother would sell me and my sister to people just so she could get her next hit. A few years later she was arrested for prostitution and drug possession and they shipped my sister and I to foster care. We ended up getting split up when she got adopted and they didn't want to take me. I went from foster home to foster home, some were good and some were bad. I knew when I turned sixteen I could be on my own so I ran away and gave my life to the streets. I fell in love with a drug dealer. We had money and I was living the life but he was controlling and he was a habitual cheater but I loved him, he was my first love. I used to move cocaine for him and now that I think about it, I use to hate my mother for doing drugs only for me to turn around and sell it to someone else's mother. How crazy was I? I was with him for about five years until I got caught selling some weed for him. They locked me up and he said since I've never been in trouble I would probably only have to do one year but when the verdict came back, I was booked for twelve years. Do you think he looked for me, nope I was out of sight and out of mind? Being in jail was what I needed, I was going down the wrong path and jail slowed me down. I did some schooling there and there was always preachers and women's group coming to the prison to encourage us and talk to us about God. I

connected with one of the preachers and he connected me
with a mentor who would mentor me while I was in
prison. After about six years I was released, the preacher
got me a lawyer who appealed my case and I won and
they let me out. It was difficult at first because I wanted to
hit the streets but my mentor stayed on me and she helped
me do right. When I was in jail I had moments of sadness,
pain. The first year there I cried all the time trying to figure
out why God would let me suffer this way. The
preacher and the mentors helped me see God in a different
light. God has truly brought me a long way. I've been a
licensed therapist for the past four years and I just opened
my own practice last year, I am married and I have a three-
year-old daughter but I wanted to tell you that no matter
how you started, you don't have to finish that way.

"Joy, I know you've been going through a lot lately. That's
why I invited you so you could meet them, because they
have helped me overcome, they both attend my church
and they were the women that helped me when I was
down.

They showed me that life can be worth living." Cyn said.

"Wow ya'll have been through a lot, and ya'll's story have
touched me. I do want better, I want to get to the end to
see how happy I would be but I don't know where to
start."

"You can start with God." Mia said.

"I just don't know, ya'll talk about your stories but how
can you not blame God for all that has happened." I said.

"Joy, I used to blame God every day when I first got locked up but then I realized I couldn't blame God for the choices humans make or the choices I make." Arielle said.

"I guess I'm not there yet because so many things happened that I wished he would have stopped." I said

"I wanted that same thing and I learned that because we have free will, sometimes bad things happen to good people as the result of the evil choices other people made and the result is you had to suffer. I learned that some unfavorable things happen to us, not for us but for our purpose in life. You suffered so you can eventually give someone else Life." Arielle said.

"I guess it's something I still have to work on because I still blame God. I be wondering do he even care." I said.

"Yes, baby God does care and he loves you but it takes time to get to that place with him. When you get to a place of healing it will all make sense." Mia said.

"I have a son, who has seen me go through so much. I just want him to see me doing better. I'm tired of going through the same stuff repeatedly."

"Now you have us, we're here to help." Cyn said.

   We continued talking about a lot of things and pulling questions out of the coffee mug. The questions were really good and pulled a lot out of me. I wished Shantel could have been here to see other women doing good. I've been given certain advice but these women have enlightened me on a deeper level about love, relationships, healing and other things. Which made me think about cutting Julian loose, I wanted love to feel good. I'm so glad Cyn invited me.

At the end of the night Cyn gave everyone a copy of this book called *"Falling in Love with Yourself"* by author *Bre'Yanna Mitriece*. Cyn said this book would help me become the person I needed to be. Arielle gave me her number and said she would be my mentor and she would counsel   me for free if I wanted it. I was think about taking her up on her offer. There were so many things I needed to work through so I could become a better person for me and for B.J. It was nice to know that I wasn't the only one who has suffered great pain, it was nice to see them and where they are now and it did give me hope that my life can get better. I hope Arielle can help find my joy.

Chapter 33

"Moving towards Healing"

"Hello, hi Joy, Mrs. Robinson would be with you shortly." The middle-aged receptionist said.

It's been about a month since Cyn's girl's night in and Fall 2015 was upon us. I really learned a lot that night. I did want better for my life. I was tired of crying and being hurt trying to chase love. I haven't cut Julian completely off yet, I was still holding on to cure my loneliness but internally I wanted to be done, I just needed to find the strength. I took Arielle up on her offer and started counseling with her. This was my third counseling session with Arielle and today she wanted us to deal with the hurt and pain of my past so I could work on healing and forgiveness.

"Mrs. Robinson will see you now." The receptionist said.

I walked back to her office and my nerves started getting the best of me. I was having mixed emotions about dealing with my past. Her door was opened and I walked in and sat on the couch. She looked nice. She had her hair pulled up in bun. She had on a black pencil skirt with a white blouse and some black pumps. She looked so much like *"Gina"* from *Martin*.

"Hey, Joy how are you today?" she said. "Are you ready for today?"

"I guess." I said hesitantly.

"Did you do your homework? Did you make your list?

"Yes, I did." I said.

"I'm going to let you hold on to it for our exercise, today we are working on Forgiveness. Remember forgiving someone isn't for them or it isn't saying you're ok with what they've done. Forgiving helps you find that peace of mind and helps heal you from being bitter, hateful and hard, when you forgive you become free. Let's start with your list, who's number one" Arielle said.

"God." I said.

"Let's talk about that, why is God first on your list?"

"Because he didn't step in and stop any of the things from happening to me." I said.

"Do you think you could forgive God?" She asked.

"Why, though. God didn't care enough for me to stop me from getting hurt and being abandoned."

"What has hating God done for you?"

"Nothing, I just can't love him."

"Let's take another look at it. What do you think would happen if you were to forgive God?"

"I don't know." I shrugged my shoulders.

"Right now, get it all out, tell God how you feel, let's work through this."

"God, where were you? Where were you? I called, you never came, you never came." Tears swelled up in my eyes. "Why did you let them hurt me and touch on me? How can I love you and you never loved me" All the emotions I had come up? Arielle handed me some Kleenex.

"Joy, God loves you more than you know and when you began to understand him you will begin to understand and see his love. He's aware of your pain and although you had to suffer, he's going to turn your pain into purpose and you will change lives because of what you've been through.

The things that happened to you were evil. God has kept you for a greater purpose. Allow him into heart and you see the him for who he is.

"I don't know, if I can." I shrugged my shoulders again.

"You can and you will but I understand forgiveness doesn't   happen in one day but the seed has been planted and when you get to that place in your healing you will forgive, who's next on your list?"

"My dad." I said.

"Talk about your dad."

"I remember my dad when I was little. I don't remember him spending much time with me he was always gone. I do remember my dad always hurting my mom with his cheating but what hurts the most" I could barely get a word out without sobbing. " It's when my Dad didn't even want me after my mom died. He never came back, he just abandoned me as if I wasn't even his. I used to hope for him to come back but then that hope became hate and I began hating him. I hated him for making my mom commit suicide and if he hadn't left me I wouldn't had to live with that monster. I can't stand my dad, he should have come back for me."

"What your Dad did wasn't right and any man should be ashamed to leave their daughter to pursue life on their own. Your dad was wrong. Your need for him has subconsciously caused you to seek out men like your father. You've dealt with men who abandoned you. If you want to have better relationships, you must begin to forgive your dad not for him because this isn't about him. This is about you, and making sure you don't continue getting into relationships with men that behave like your father. Go ahead and cry. Let it all out." Arielle said.

Arielle allowed me to cry for a little while my dad has hurt me and it still stings. I don't want him controlling me anymore or me dating men like him. I just wished my daddy knew how that one decision he made how it changed the course of my life.

"Are you ready to move on to the next person, who next?" Arielle asked.

"My mom." I said sobbing. I broke down. "I can't do this Arielle."

"Yes, you can Joy, you have to face the hard parts so you can heal. Why do you hate your mom?"

"Like, I mean did she not love me enough. Why wasn't I good enough, why did she leave me when she knew my daddy was out doing his own thing. I just don't understand how a mother could just leave her child behind. Why did she abandon me?"

I tried to wipe my tears but they kept flowing from my eyes. I took a deep breath. My breathing got heavy. I tried to get myself together.

"I don't want to hate her but at times I do. Sometimes I'm angry and sometimes I'm sad. I was her only child, didn't she has any more fight left for me. She just let my daddy take all the life out of her and I miss her, I miss her so much. I just wish I could touch her again." I said wiping the tears from my eyes.

"Your mom loved you but some people don't know how to cope with pain that is detrimental to them. Some people see suicide as the only coping method that will relieve the pain they're feeling. She was in pain and she wanted out. She was severely depressed and she was wrapped up in her own pain that she didn't commit suicide because she didn't love you, she committed suicide because she wanted to get rid of her pain. She didn't think about the effect of her suicide she just wanted to end the pain. What she did to its effect on you, your mom had her own issues outside of you and she didn't know how to handle them. You must forgive your mom, so you can free yourself from reliving her life. Depression is real and unfortunately before your mom got any help it was already too late." Arielle said.

I took another deep breath and the tears were still flowing. I needed to forgive my mother. I've been there before so hurt and in pain that death does seem so much better and after catching my dad continuously cheating guess she just couldn't take it anymore. While suicide isn't the answer, I can now put myself in her shoes and understand why she may have done it.

"Are you ready to move on? Who's next?"

"My grandparents." I said wiping my eyes.

"Why do you hate them?"

"They were just evil, my grandma turned a blind eye when my grandpa was molesting me. She didn't help me at all, how do you let a grown man touch your grandchild and you do nothing about it. My grandpa is a sick bastard and he died a while ago and I couldn't be happier. He destroyed my life. He took away a piece of me I could never get back. They didn't care nothing about me even though I was their daughter's child. They just pushed me off on somebody else and they abandoned me. I've always wondered if my struggles with sex stems from my molestation. I never valued my body. I gave it up to any guy that showed interest. My grandparents are the scum on the earth." I said.

"What your grandparents did was beyond evil and he should have been put in jail behind it. Some people molest because they are victims of molestation and they just pass it down and pass it down until someone finally stand up and stop it. I know you want nothing to do with them and I agree and I know that forgiving them will take some time. Take as much time as you need." Arielle said.

I burst out crying again. "Arielle I've just been hurt and that's just the tip of the iceberg.

"Joy just by doing what you've started doing we are on the road towards your healing and growth and freedom, so we have to do the hard stuff, open that old wound so we can heal it the right way, I'm going to send home some more exercises for you to do at home for those on your list, who's next." Arielle said.

"Me."

"You? Why do you hate you?"

"I've never been the pretty girl or have the perfect body. I've just never felt good enough or loveable and I guess I hate myself for all the stuff I 've done. I hate my life at times. I hate being Joy." I said.

"Joy forgiveness works for you to. You must forgive yourself for some of your past choices. That's the first step to loving you. Then we must strengthen your self-esteem, build it up. I have a worksheet for you to help boost you up, so you can learn to love you. I'm going to be with you the whole way through. Joy I'm going to give you these worksheets and I want you to do them so we could discuss them when you come back as we continue to work on forgiveness and your healing. Here are those papers and here are some bible verses for you." Arielle said.

She hands me several pieces of papers.

"Oh, and at the bottom of that paper say that daily. Say, I'm working on forgiving me and or blank. Not for him/her but for me. So, I can heal and be set free. Remember Joy change starts within and you made the first step by coming here. I'm so proud of you. We want to get you healthy so you can start attracting the right kind of relationships in your life, next week will continue to work on forgiveness and talk about your past relationships with men so you can heal in that area as well." Arielle said.

I wiped my eyes. "Thanks Arielle for everything for letting me come to you for free and helping get better.

"You're welcome, anything to see my sister getting healed." Arielle said.

"I'm just ready to be free." I said.

"You will be." She said.

We exchanged hugs and I left the office and stopped by the receptionist desk and scheduled my appointment for next week.

When I got into the car my eyes were puffy and red. I was crying a lot but it was needed. I wanted to be free like Arielle and Mia and Cyn. I wanted to happy and not stressed all the time about a man. I turned on the radio and drove down the highway to pick B.J up from his after-care program. After dinner and after B.J was in bed. I grabbed Arielle's sheet with the three bible verses and decided to read them. This was a first for me reading bible verses. I was a little apprehensive but I did want things to change in my life and Arielle has really made an impact on me and if she could change her life after all she went through I wanted to do the same. I didn't even own a bible but the verses were all written on the sheet and a description of each verse. It helped because I knew nothing about the bible. I pulled the sheet out and read it.

Bible Verses to help move you towards Healing

Luke 23:34

"Then said Jesus, Father forgive them for they know not what they do."

There are some people who hurt other people and they really don't know the extent of the pain they have caused. They are ignorant to the fact that they are a hurt person hurting other people. Jesus want us to forgive those who hurt us not to excuse their action but because they are ignorant to the pain they have caused and so we don't let the pain they have caused us to keep us bounded up but we forgive so we can eventually move beyond the pain.

Ephesians 4:31-32

"Get rid of all the bitterness, rage, anger, brawling and slander, along with every form of malice. Be compassionate to one another, forgiving others as Christ God forgave you."

Get rid of all those things from your heart because they are weighing you down and you can't move forward because you're dragging around that baggage. Bags of bitterness. Bags of hate and anger. Let it all go and forgive whomever have made you feel that way because being kind and compassionate when you meet new people is so much better than carrying around hate and bitterness.

Colossians 1:13-14

"For he has rescued us from the dominion of darkness and brought us into the kingdom of the Son he loves, in who we have redemption, the forgiveness of sins."

You no longer have to hate yourself for what you've done in the past or for who you use to be, God has forgiven you for all your past transgressions. God has rescued you from that old weary life and brought you into a life with Christ, where you are now walking in light and freedom.

At the bottom of the page it said to meditate on these daily; All sudden I started crying. I don't know what came over me but the tears kept flowing. I grabbed the other sheet and repeated.

"I'm working on forgiving my mom, not for her but for me so I could be set free."

I repeated the saying adding in my dad's name, my grandparent's names and some of the men I dealt with names. The tears kept coming, but Arielle said crying was good and that crying was necessary for my healing. In the mist of crying I noticed out the corner of my eye the book "*Falling In love with Yourself*". I haven't had a chance to read it since I received it from Cyn. I was already full of emotions and I decided to open the book and read it. I opened the book and the first page I turned to was about forgiveness and going to God. I continued to read chapter after chapter, it was like this book was written for me. I finished the book in one setting and everything Arielle was helping me with the book also highlighted some of those same things.

I learned a lot from the book and what loving myself really looks like and I was learning that I had a long way to go but as long as I keep walking towards better things, it's only a matter of time before they come and I wanted to keep walking this time. I grabbed the positive affirmation sheet Arielle gave me and worked on that a bit, it felt strange speaking to myself and pumping myself up because I've always talked down to myself. I couldn't help but cry during this exercise because I had to call myself beautiful and smart and other words that I never assigned to me but Arielle challenged me to speak positivity over myself and my life and any negative thought had to be replace with a positive thought.

This way of living is all new to me, but I want it, I desperately need to continue moving towards healing.

Chapter 34

"Joy comes in the Morning"

"I am Beautiful, I am smart, I am healed, I am worthy of love. I will overcome, I will be a great mother, I will love myself." I repeated my positive affirmations as I stared at my reflection in the mirror, a reflection I was learning to love.

Over the past six months I have been on a journey of self-discovery. Some days were a struggle but I made it through. I have continued counseling with Arielle and she has been a big help in where I am in my life today. Counseling has helped me face the unresolved issues in my life and has helped me find my breakthrough, find something call peace and find my healing. I've learned accountability and I've learned that I'm no longer the victim but I am victorious.

I continued to hold on to Julian for a while but Arielle helped me see that men where my greatest challenge and I held on to men because of my fear of being alone and abandoned. I kept Julian around even though I knew he wasn't good for me, I held on to him so I wouldn't have to feel like someone left me again. Arielle encouraged me to let him go and it was hard. I had to stop the communication and cut him off from sex. She suggested that I changed my number so he wouldn't have access to me. I did what she advised and in those moments where I craved him, she told me to call her instead. I had a few slip ups but as of today, I have been free from Julian for the past three months. I take it one day at a time, but I am happy he's out of my life.

When I finally let, Julian go, I didn't know which way to go and Arielle wanted me to try to be alone for a season. She wanted me to do something I've never done so I can heal and learn to love my own company so I could stop revolving my life around unhealthy men. She suggested I do a 90 day no-man fast where I focus on God, and healing and growing myself. I'm currently doing that now and I am 22 days into my fast and it's different but I know it's necessary for my growth. I began journaling and I started finding new hobbies that peaked my interest.

I'm coming along with my beauty and the tips Arielle gave me and the tips from the book "*Falling in love with Yourself*" has helped me. I'm not where I want to be but I'm much better than I used to be. I don't beat   myself down or say negative things to myself like I use to. I speak positive things about my beauty daily.

I finally took Cyn up on her offer a few months ago to attend her church. I really enjoyed her church, they were so friendly and the Pastor was down to earth and funny. Some of my sessions with Arielle were all about God. She helps me pray and she helps me understand the bible in a deeper way. She has worked with me on figuring out my purpose in this life. I have learned how to pray on my own and I read the bible often. I have learned to trust God and his plan for my life and know that he is with me always.

Shantel is still hanging on to Desmond and I gave her my copy of the book *"Falling in love with Yourself"* so she can see she doesn't have to live that way but she isn't ready yet and Arielle said people must be ready to change, you can't force them to want change, they must want it on their own. So now I pray for her and I pray that one day she finds her strength so she can go after her better. We don't hang out like we use to but she will always be my sister.

Bridgette finally got married to her man Quan and she is now pregnant with a little girl. She is going back to school for cosmetology. She has made a lot of changes from who she uses to be and she is going after her better. I'm so proud of her.

Cyn still sends me inspirational messages every day and they mean more to me now than they ever did. She is doing well and she is writing a book about her journey. I am so grateful for her because she wants the best for me. She has been one of the main people in my corner encouraging me, letting me know I can have better. I looked at myself in the mirror and thanked God for being where I am today. About a month ago, On March 14, 2016, I gave my life to God and today I am getting baptized. I shed a few tears as I stare at my reflection again in the mirror.

Arielle and I partnered together to start a non-profit to help women who have suffered from molestation, and domestic violence. Never in a million years did I think I would be in the position to help women. Cyn has also encouraged me to tell my story, she said I should write a book. She helped me through the process and I have a book in the works detailing my life and how I made it over.

All my life I've been wondering why my mother named me Joy because my life has been anything but that. I've been hurt by others unwillingly and I have willingly let people hurt me. Today I understand that Joy also means triumph and that is what I have done. I have triumphed over everything that tried to kill me, break me and destroy me. I have triumphed over those who have abandoned me. I am Joy. I have Joy. I am finally free. A girl who grew up like I did can finally have better. Each day is a new day to love myself even more. After all my weeping, my Joy finally came in the morning and it feels so good.

Abandoned

Joy

Bre'Yanna Mitriece

If you are suffering from any type of abuse. Please reach out to the:

 Domestic Violence Hotline 1-800-799-7233 or 1-800-787-3224(TTY)

Mailing Address: The National Domestic Violence Hotline P.O Box 161810 Austin, TX,78716

*If you are battling with suicide. Please reach out to the:

National Suicide Prevention Lifeline 1-800-273-8255

Your life matters

*If you want to give your life to Christ, just read this simple verse and you will be Saved.

"If you declare with your mouth," Jesus is Lord," and believe in your heart that God raised him from the dead, you will be saved. For it is with your heart that you believe and are justified, and it is with your mouth that you profess your faith and are saved."

Romans 10:9-10

After Salvation plant, yourself in a bible-based church that preaches and teaches the unadulterated word of God to further your walk with God. Spend time in a secret place getting to know God Personally.

If you're tired of being stuck and ready to go after your better.

Are you ready to make some real and permanent changes?

Email:

Breyanna@Breyannamitriece.com for more information

www.ingramcontent.com/pod-product-compliance
Lightning Source LLC
Chambersburg PA
CBHW060946030726
47503CB00003B/750